A BEACH READ

A THIRD ROMEO AFFAIR

With Matt, Ashley and the General

A Novel By

HARRY KATZAN JR.

Author's Tranquility Press
ATLANTA, GEORGIA

Copyright © 2024 by Harry Katzan Jr.

All rights reserved. No part of this publication may be reproduced, distributed or transmitted in any form or by any means, including photocopying, recording, or other electronic or mechanical methods, without the prior written permission of the publisher, except in the case of brief quotations embodied in critical reviews and certain other noncommercial uses permitted by copyright law. For permission requests, write to the publisher, addressed "Attention: Permissions Coordinator," at the address below.

Harry Katzan Jr./Author's Tranquility Press
3900 N Commerce Dr. Suite 300 #1255
Atlanta, GA 30344
www.authorstranquilitypress.com

Ordering Information:
Quantity sales. Special discounts are available on quantity purchases by corporations, associations, and others. For details, contact the "Special Sales Department" at the address above.

A Third Romeo Affair/Harry Katzan Jr.
Hardback: 978-1-963636-58-1
Paperback: 978-1-963636-59-8
eBook: 978-1-963636-60-4

OTHER Beach Reads BY HARRY KATZAN, JR.

The Romeo Affair

Another Romeo Affair

Up, Down and Anywhere

Here, There and Everywhere

For Margaret, with all my love
now and forever

INTRODUCTION

Matt and the General are at it again, but this time it is collection of short stories from various sources. The subject matter is paraphrased to make for easy reading. It is written so that various members of the Romeo Club can tell an interesting story. Matt, Ashley, the General, and Anna are involved, as usual, and the setting is amusing and informative.

The setting is the Romeo Club, that is, the Retired Old Men Eating Out club. The men meet on the first and third Wednesday of the month to have breakfast, and hopefully to discuss the news of the day and whatever else they want to talk about.

In the Romeo Club, the membership is primarily retired men but other persons, such as retired women and younger men and women are welcomed. One of the characteristics of the Romeo Club is, in some sense, all of the men are equal, after they retire. The members are doctors, lawyers, professors, company presidents, White House employees, and so forth, as long as they are residents of Sun City, an up-scale gated community adjacent to Hilton Head Island in South Carolina, a community primarily composed of wealthy retired people

Matthew (Matt) Miller is a distinguished math professor at a distinguished university; the General is a retired military general who is wealthy from a prosperous business company; Ashley, Matt's wife, is a former movie star that teaches drama at a local community college; and Anna, whose given name is Marguerite Purgoine, a retired professor of creative writing.

This edition is a sequel to the first edition of a book entitled *The Romeo Affair* and the second edition that is entitled *Another Romeo Affair.*

The scene changes rapidly, but always in the scope of no violence, no sex, and no bad language. It is amenable to all age groups. The book typifies the conventional "beach" read in that the subject matter can be read as a collection of separate stories. The basic idea behind the book is that reading is fun.

The early chapters start slowly so as not to give all of the good stuff at the beginning. Each chapter is independent of the others and can be read in any order.

Chapters 8 and 20 are related and should be given some attention; you will enjoy the finale to each chapter. If you are tired and want a rest, we have Chapter 24, Just in Case.

It is only fair to mention that the stories are short because, after all, it is intended to be a beach read, and many of the details are not given. If you would like to know more, the library at the end will come to your rescue.

This is a book in the Matt and the General series. The characters assume their dynamic personalities as in previous tales.

The Author,
February 2024

MAIN CHARACTERS IN THE BOOK

The General – Les Miller. Former military General and Humanitarian. P-51 pilot and World War II hero.

Matthew (Matt) Miller – Professor of Mathematics. Grandson of the General. Sophisticated problem solver and strategist.

Ashley Wilson Miller – College friend of Matt Miller. Married to Matt Miller. Receiver of the National Medal of Freedom.

Marguerite Purgoine - Retired creative writing Professor and an associate of the team. Known as Anna for some unknown reason. Wife of the General.

Sir Charles (Buzz) Bunday – P-51 pilot and Army Air Force buddy of Les Miller. Member of the British Security Service. Knight of the United Kingdom.

General Clark – Mark Clark, Former Four Star General and Chairman of the Joint Chiefs of Staff, Appointed to be U.S. Director of Intelligence.

Ann Clark – Wife of General Clark and associate of the team. Formerly combat colonel in the U.S. Army.

Kimberly Scott – The Intelligence specialist of the U.S. Has an extensive publications record.

Katherine Penelope Radford – Retired Queen of the United Kingdom and personal friend of the General.

Adam Benfield – Iranian terrorist leader known as Atalus. Spy for the U.S. and England.

Maya Wilson – Member of the ladies Fab Five quilting group and government analyst.

Kenneth Strong – President of the United States.

Elizabeth Strong – Wife of Kenneth Strong and is First Lady of the United States.

George Benson – Associate to the President and Chief of Staff.

Harry Steevens – Expert mathematician and former college friend of Matt Miller. Policeman in Hilton Head.

Wuan Singh – Chinese mathematician.

Prince Michael (Davis) – Son of the queen and astrophysicist

Harp Thomas – Academic friend of Matt and professor of mathematics in Switzerland.

Kimberly Jobsen Thomas – Wife of Harp Thomas and banking consultant.

Robert Peterson – Iranian director of technology. Former student associate of the General.

Steve Smith – Director of the Romeo Club.

Adam Benfield – Iranian/U.S. terrorist leader known Atalus.

And a few others

Contents

CHAPTER 1

Return to Inaction

The ride home in the electric plane was very solemn. They had been given the usual thank you, the expected medal of freedom, and an offer of a polite luncheon that was not accepted. To the General it was, "Case closed," We all need a vacation in Hawaii that was refused by the others. As they say, it was Deja Vue all over again.

"We just need a period of inactivity," said Matt. "We have been going at top speed for too long. We need a long rest."

"That's what I say," replied Ashley. "It was not like we were doing what we like to do; we were doing what we had to do. All I want to do is to have my hair done, have a nice dinner, and just watch a little TV."

"A little golf and a nice dinner is all that I need," answered the General. "And a good night's sleep."

"Well, that's it then," said Matt. "I see the handwriting on the wall. The General and I play a comfortable round of golf while you are getting your hair done, we have a pleasant dinner, and maybe a little TV. Probably an older movie would be good, not too much action, and maybe a little popcorn if we're still hungry."

"You are always hungry," said Ashley.

*****

The next morning at 6:00 am the phone rang. Matt slept right through it and Ashley pretended it never happened. At 7:00 it rang again and Ashley answered.

"Good morning General, how are you this fine morning?" answered Ashley.

"I'm just fine," said the General. "It's a fine day for golf, and I am calling to see if Matt would be interested at about 10:00, as usual."

"It must be fine day," said Matt to Ashley. "Please say that would be fine with me if it is fine with you."

"Matt says it will be fine, General," replied Ashley, who hung up the phone and rolled over for another 15 minutes or so of fine sleep.

"I can't believe it," murmured Matt as he also rolled over for a few fine minutes of sleep.

*****

At the ninth hole, Matt and the General stopped for a brief chat. Both men were just plain tired.

"We need to get out of here," said the General. "We need a change for a few days, if not longer."

"Are you thinking of Sun City?" asked Matt.

"Actually, I was," said the General. "It has good golf courses in the area and Ashley has that group of quilters she calls the Fab Five. We could go to the Romeo Club and see what's going on down there."

"How would we get down there?" asked Matt. "I don't feel like driving all the way down there; the traffic is horrible these days. Could we fly down? We have a car down there."

"We could and have that Iranian guy pick us up," replied the General. "He really liked us; he thinks we turned his life around. I neglected to tell you that Clark in his position of Director of Intelligence granted him a U.S. citizenship and also got him a professorship at that university in upper New Jersey. Not only that, he is a full professor. He is a big story. He has an American girlfriend. They are going to be married."

"What is he teaching?" asked Matt.

"Artificial Intelligence," answered the General. "Apparently those Iranians must be smarter than Americans think they are."

"Americans think they are the only people with brains," continued Matt. "The people from all over – Germany, England, Switzerland, Russia, and so forth – are just a smart as Americans. Maybe smarter."

And so it came to be that Ashley, Matt, and the General flew to Hilton Head Island in the General's small plane and were met at the Hilton Head Airport by Dr. Adam Benfield, formerly a spy with the name Atalus, in his favorite car, a beautiful Mercedes S500 sedan. The meeting was joyous, they all liked each other.

END OF CHAPTER ONE

CHAPTER 2

How About the Romeo Club

On the ride from the Hilton Head Airport to Sun City, Adam Benfield was literally bursting with excitement. At every pause in the conversation, Adam tried to get a word in but was drowned out. Finally he got the microphone, as people say, and here is what he had to say.

"I talked to my girlfriend this morning and she says that she knows you – all of you," he said, "the General, Matt, and Ashley."

"Well spit it out Adam," said Matt. "We are sitting here on pins and needles waiting to hear what you have to say."

"Her name is Maya Wilson," replied Adam. "She say says she worked with you and is a quilting partner of Ashley. She mentioned the Fab Five, and that is all she said about you."

"Well, I'll be," said Matt.

"She says she liked me even better than you Matt," said Adam.

"Whew, I was worried about that," replied Matt. "Couldn't sleep for two nights." That got a laugh out of Ashley.

"You can cut that out," said the General. "You know you liked Maya Wilson and you are fond of Dr. Benfield."

"I'm sorry," said Matt. "I'm just tired of being so careful after dealing with all of those stuffy government people."

"It's okay Matt," replied Adam Benfield. "That's just the way that I feel. It's sometimes a real pain in the you know what. I have a message for you General from Mr. Steve Smith. He would like you to call him."

"How does he know that I am/will be here?" asked the General.

"I told him," answered Adam. "I hope that wasn't a mistake."

"He wanted you to do that Adam," said Ashley. "The General loves the Romeo club, and so do the rest of us."

"This is really a nice car Adam," said Matt. "Is it brand new?"

"It's five years old," replied Adam. "The German cars are the best. I once rode on the Autobahn at 150 miles per hour, and it was like a dream."

*****

"You've called Steve Smith, leader of the prestigious Romeo Club in Sun City," answered Steve Smith's phone. "Hello, Les, I'm glad you called."

"I just called to see what is going on," answered the General. "We have been unusually busy. A person just does what they have to do. We are here now. What's going on?"

"We have had a few incidents like you had with that New York doctor," answered Smith. "One guy who was an Army dentist thought he was better than another guy with 2 PhDs, a JD, and worked in the U.S. State Department. In another incident, a muscle-bound NFL player lauded over a guy who had finished over 100 marathons. In yet another case a person who had been a company president couldn't stand a former college professor who had written more than 50 books, 100 papers, and had one patent. So I had to make a formal rule to the effect that all Romeo members and other attendees were equal in the eyes of the club. We had to set the fixed price for the breakfast no matter how much or how little they ate. No alcohol beverages are allowed, even though I and most members would have imagined that was not needed. The members repeatedly asked for programs like you and Matt made up and agreed that an informal discussion of unusual things that happened to members or members knew about could be interesting. Especially unique events that happened to older persons. The next meeting is this coming Wednesday and we would hope you would attend. By the way, we have an interesting new members who mentioned that he had been a spy as a career and now was a valid citizen of the US and is currently a professor of Artificial Intelligence. You guys know about that AI stuff that appears to be a hot topic these days. Does that answer your question? I'm only kidding."

"Matt and I will be there and will be looking forward to it," answered the General.

*****

“Well Matt, I talked with Steve Smith and they would be pleased to have us attend the next Romeo Club meeting,” said the General.” We don’t have to do anything but perhaps in the future it could be appropriate to do something for the club. Another thing, they have had or are going to have something new to the Romeo Club. Members could describe interesting thing that happened to them or they had heard about. Some of those events we experience are quite interesting when viewed afterwards. Especially when the events are not personal.”

END OF CHAPTER TWO

CHAPTER 3

Interesting Events

Steve Smith must have sent an email to all active members, because the turnout was better than ever before. The manager at Bono's had to assign two extra tables, but he was more than pleased to do it. Matt and the General were pleased. Ashley and Maya decided to take their breakfast next door.

"Where are the girls?" asked Smith.

"They are next door," said the General. "They thought we needed our privacy."

"Bring them in. Bring them in," said Smith. "The men love them. I'll have the Bono's manager get them in here."

As it was, Ashley and Maya received a loud ovation when they walked in the front door. The breakfast was delicious, as usual, the everyone sat back in their chairs, ready for the show.

Steve Smith had to make an explanation that Matt and the General had just returned and did not have timer to work something up. A gentleman in that back said, 'Let's do some of that 'interesting event' idea that we made up in the last meeting."

The most vocal meeting of the club was about to start.

"I'll write the title of each idea on the blackboard we have here; someone might want to copy the subjects down," said Smith.

The End

Allen Brown, at the rear, immediate came up with, "Everything will be all right in the end. If it is not, then it is not the end." The idea generated nothing but blank stares.

Teamwork

George Richards, right in front, responded with, "It takes teamwork to make a dream work." Most people just yawned. Was all of this a good idea?

Security

Jim Hefner, started out by standing up, and moving his chair back. He was ready. "I have a friend whose son worked for the big aircraft company in the northwest. It is a high security employer because of government/military work. The son worked for 6 months on the mathematics to solve some problem such as guiding missiles or drones or something. He went to graduate school and came back to work there. He was curious about the work he had done previously. It was secret and he couldn't even see it because he did not have a need to know."

"I can beat that said James Grey. Documents were either secret or confidential. To read a security document, you had to have a secret clearance. It was an involved process. To read confidential documents, you only needed a credit check by the Army. At night, secret documents had to be returned to the security library. Confidential documents only had to be placed in a drawer out of sight. My son had checked out a confidential document and another employee asked to look at it. The next morning my son got to work and the place was a quiet as a mouse. Someone had a security violation and would probably be fired, and possibly sent to prison. It was my son. The other employee returned the document after working hours, and just threw it on the top of my son's desk. Company security came around and bingo, a security violation that was very uncommon. My son was called into his manager's office and was asked what had happened. My son explained, and he was not fired. The protocol changed and all confidential documents had to be returned during the work day."

"You sounded like a professor," someone said. "I was," said Grey.

"Any more security?" asked Smith. "Then we can move on."

"I have a short one," said Joe Richards. "Our son worked there also. He was 21 and just out of college. The company had just received a big government contract and hired a large number of employees of the same age. They were all single and alone, for the most part, and met in a small restaurant near the plant, usually on Sunday nights. One Sunday, an Air Force officer and a handful of armed guards came in to arrest the boys. They thought they were a spying group. Fortunately, the officer was also a young guy, only two years older than our son. They attended the same university and majored in math. They recognized each other, our son explained the situation, and the arrests were averted. Can you imagine how afraid the young guys must have been?"

The Flat Tire

"I have what I think is a good example of that security work environment," said Richard Evans. "When you work on government contracts, it possible to have contract cancellations and employee layoffs. How should it be done? If you lay off only workers than when a new contract is received, you have no one to do the work. If you lay off only managers, then you have no one to guide the workers. So you have a totem pole and an employee's position on the totem pole is determined by education, experience, age, evaluation, and so forth. I was high on the totem pole, and my position was higher than my immediate manager. On one very busy morning, traffic on an overpass was blocked up and I got a flat tire. What to do? I had never changed a tire before. The man in the car behind me jumped out of his car to assist. He was nicely dressed but not too fancy. He said, "I'll take care of it for you," and he did. I said, "Can I give you something?" He said no, it was his job, and I remembered that. Remember I was about 22 or 23 years old and kind of a babe in the woods. When I got to work late, I told my manager that I had a flat tire and he said, "I know." And that was it. Only later did I realize that I was being tailed by a security person to safeguard employees high on the totem pole from any kind of misfortune. Employees were valuable. The government contracts were strict and bomber planes were necessary and if a plane were one day late, they would be fined a million dollars. Of course, the money in the contracts was huge. There is more to the story. Many of the assemblies were outsourced to other firms and countries. They could have problems. That is the way it is. Accordingly, every single part on an aircraft could be built in-house by an enormous manufacturing facility. It was perhaps a little less efficient than buying subcontracted parts, but they could be built in-house to meet a deadline. And that is the end of a long story. The men in the audience just looked at each other with amazement. Richard Evans got a round of applause.

"Is that true?" asked Matt.

"Sure is," replied the General.

High School Football

"I have one, but don't know how interesting it is," said Jimmy Bloom.

"Go ahead Jimmy," said someone in the rear of the breakfast area.

"I was a little squirt," said Jimmy, "and I'm not big today. "There was about 200 boys trying out for the team, but in spite of the large turnout, I made the team. I think I made the team because I could be the kicker in spite of my size. That is the way the assistant coach did business; he was an educator. Everyone knew that. One of the boys had a heart murmur and couldn't play. His father, a hot shot lawyer went to the coach who immediately said he could be on the team as the kicker, and was he lousy. I was a tail back and couldn't see over the line to throw a pass, and sat on the bench. Next year, I was off to college and the kicker was a kid of my size that lived on the next street, and was he successful. The first boy's hot shot father probably slipped a $100 or so to the coach."

"That's a tough way to learn a lesson," said someone on the first table.

Cigarettes During the War

"I have one," said Hank Goodenough. Steve Smith just nodded.

"It was in World War II and a lot of things were rationed in order to help the soldiers. One of the items that was not rationed but in short supply were cigarettes. They were distributed through the grocery stores. The notion of a supermarket was not yet in vogue. A woman when paying for her merchandize would ask the cashier if she had any cigarettes and would customarily get a no. The cashier was an enormous woman who was the laughing stock of the neighborhood. Her name was Frieda. The kids would laugh and say that she could never get a husband. About then there was a guy in the neighborhood that was as skinny as possible and more than a bit ugly to boot. His name was Roger, and he was 4-F. The neighborhood kids all called him 'Mister 6-F'. The kids laughed and said that when Roger went through the checkout line, Frieda would have cigarettes. And, she did. A short time later, they were married."

The same person at the first table said, "There is always an easy way to solve a problem."

Steve Smith ended the breakfast with a little smile. It seems as though the interesting events were not so interesting. We can do better, he thought. He looked over at the General who didn't even have a little smile.

END OF CHAPTER THREE

CHAPTER 4

The General

The director of the Romeo Club called the General. "Hi Les, how is it going where you are?"

"Not bad Steve," answered the General. "We are just resting up after our last job on this demon named Artificial Intelligence. It's got the world in a tizzy. Matt seems to have it figured out with deep learning and neural networks and says it is not that bad. All a person needs is a little bit of knowledge and a lot of work."

"The reason I called is that session we had last Wednesday did not go over all that well," said Steve Smith. "They said that there wasn't enough meat to it. I think they meant it was trivial."

"I think so too," said the General. "I think it is time to bring in Matt. He knows a lot and is a born speaker. He likes to do it. I think you want me to bring him on, and I agree. I'll have to ask him, and I guarantee that he will agree to give an informative session. On the last meeting, I think the idea was good, but the speakers should have done some preparation, and is so doing, they would come up with some interesting insights."

“Sounds good,” said Steve. “I have a meeting and have to run. See you in two weeks less one day.”

The General called Matt directly who agreed without a hesitation. The General was careful not to ask what the talk would be about, but he had the suspicion that it would be himself, the General.

*****

The breakfast entrée for the next Romeo meeting was a baked potato loaded with egg, cheese, and some veggies. The bread was exotic Palmer House rolls fashioned by the Palmer House restaurant in Boston. There were unlimited rolls, butter, and special Swiss coffee. The men loved it, since it was something they did not normally get at home. It was certainly better than a bowl of bran flakes and one slice of 70 calorie white bread.

*****

Steve Smith introduced Mat with great pleasure knowing he would make up for the previous weeks presentations.

Matt was his normal cheerful self, promising a short but interesting summary of the life and accomplishments of his grandfather the General. The entire room sat back in their chairs and stretched their legs out in front of them.

“Here is a snapshot of exactly who we are talking about when we refer to the General in the ensuing dialog. He is a retired three-star general officer who achieved a rank of Lieutenant General in the U.S. Army. In civilian life he is referred to as *The General,* because of his record of accomplishment in and out of the military. He holds bachelors, masters, and doctorate degrees and is the founder of a prestigious political polling company.

The General, whose given name is Les Miller and his wing man Charles (Bizz) Bunday were First Lieutenants in the Army Air Force who had completed their required number of 25 missions as P-51 support pilots that accompanied B-17 bomber runs in World War II. Most fighter pilots were shot down before they could complete their required number of missions. The two lieutenants were ordered to report to the commander and received their promotions to Captain, given two weeks leave, and ordered to report to the Pentagon for duty or assignment.

The two pilots enjoyed their two weeks leave in New York City, along with a fine hotel and good food. Buzz, born and raised in England, was amazed by the quality of life in what many Englanders refer to as the colonies.

At the Pentagon, Captain Miller and Captain Bunday were ordered to report to a high-level secret meeting concerning the number of P-51s shot down in a single mission, which is roughly 60%. The commanders of the U.S. and Britain believe that a failure rate that high could not be sustained in terms of personnel and equipment.

The Air Force tried titanium panels as armament and the method did not work. So, the big guns were brought in to solve the problem. The meeting was being attended by three-star generals, college professors, and noted scientists. The problem was well defined. All of the bullet holes were covered up but the planes continue to be shot down. Captain Les Miller says, "I can solve the problem." Buzz said, "Les, are you out of your mind? You're probably going to get us demoted."

Les replied, "Don't worry Buzz, I'll solve the problem."

Captain Miller was asked to describe the method that he says will solve the problem. Here is Miller's response. "The objective of the meeting is to determine where titanium plates are to be placed for protection of P-51s. Here are some photos." The photos showed P-51s with bullet holes. "The planes have been plated where the holes are with no improvement. Now, that is the reason why we are here. It's an easy problem." Captain Miller calmly continued, "It's easy gentlemen. The important holes went down with the plane – in fact, probably caused it. Look at the photos, do you see any planes with holes in the bellies, for example. We should plating areas where there is no holes. If the Army Air Force would armor plate the untouched areas evident in the photos we have, the problem will be solved," said Miller.

The armor plating was placed in clean aircraft bellies, and the percent of shot down planes was reduced to 10%. Note, this is an actual true story. Captain Miller, and his buddy Bunday were promoted forthwith to the rank of Major. Again, this is a true story. I have researched it and read the descriptive math paper that describes it. The reference is Ellenberg, J., *How Not to Be Wrong: The power of Mathematical Thinking,* New York: The Penquin Press, 2014, pp. 5-8. Ellenberg gives the scientist as Abraham Wald and name of the mathematical concept is *survivorship bias.* A professor worked on it for some time.

There is one more description of the General and how he eventually and implicitly inherited the title of General. As is commonly the case, an Army officer must obtain a promotion within a certain time period. If there is no open slot, then he or she must retire as an officer. That is the Army way. Once out of the service, the General called his friend Bill Donovan from the Nuremburg war trials. Donovan defended Gary Powers in the famous World War II trial and eventually became President of a university in Brooklyn, New York. Donovan said to General Miller, "I was once in your position Les, why don't you come to my university and get an M.S. in computer Science? We have one of the finest masters programs in the world, if not the first, on the subject." The General did just that, getting his MS degree and meeting some Iranian students, one of which is portrayed in other episodes.

The General used the knowledge he obtained from his MS degree in Computer Science to build a large political polling company. He gained an enormous fortune and gained the reputation as a person who used his wealth to help people.

The General eventually received his PhD in International Relations, as an officer in the Army, where the time and money for his studies was granted for outstanding personal achievement. That is the Army way.

The General was and is an avid golfer which he and his grandson Dr. Matt Miller played at least twice in a week. The General also established an upscale restaurant named the *Green Room*, that he used for business and pleasure.

The General owns a personal aircraft named the Gulfstream 650 that was purchased with personal money. A few years later, he obtained a small business jet for short trips. The General has numerous friends in the Army. One of which is General Mark Clark, four-star Chief of Staff, and eventually

Director of Intelligence. The General is also the friend of the President and the First Lady.

One more thing. After the P-51 problem was resolved, Major Les Miller's new job was straightforward. All it amounted to was to check returning P-51 flights and perform an assessment of damage from interactions with the enemy, go to the next air base and do the same thing. The plan was more than obvious. After changes are completed, he would certify deployment and analyze returning flights to insure the protective measures were working. The travel between bases in England was treacherous and often involved travel over muddy roads. When a trip was lengthy, it necessitated sleeping in a pup tent and eating K rations. Actually, the K rations weren't that bad and the kit usually contained a chocolate bar and a pack of Lucky Strike cigarettes. The officers also had nylon stockings to give to the local residents. The relationship between U.S. servicemen and English country folk was usually quite pleasant.

Miller's driver, a Master Sergeant, was a likeable fellow, and he and Miller got along splendidly. Along one long stretch of muddy road, they came upon a young woman who had slipped off the read while driving a light military truck. Actually, Miller driven by his driver passed by her for security reasons and then returned to offer assistance. It turned out that she was a Second Subattern (i.e., a second lieutenant) in the women's Auxiliary Territorial Service. Her specialty was mechanics and truck driving. Assisting with the war effort was an honorable thing to do for women at that time in history.

"Are you okay?" asked Miller.

"I'm okay," she answered. "I'm just a bit frightened. I've been off the road for a long while and thought that no one come by up to assist me. You are Americans?"

"We are both Americans," answered Miller. "Let us help you."

The jeep, a remarkable little vehicle, pulled her out of the mud, and the conversation continued.

"We are traveling to the RAF Grangemouth air base," continued Miller. "We work on airplanes."

"You are a Colonel. Do you fly airplanes?" The pretty young woman asked. "My name is Mary Wales, by the way."

"I am a pilot," answered Miller. "My name is Les Miller and my driver is Sergeant Bud Small. By the way, would you like some chocolate, or cigarettes or nylons? We have chocolate and cigarettes from our K rations, and they give us nylons to give to women that we encounter. We know that some items are not available in England."

"I would appreciate some chocolate and nylons. I'm very hungry and have been waiting here – off the road for a long time."

"Are you sure you don't want cigarettes?" asked Bud.

"No thank you, I don't smoke," said Mary. "Smoking is bad for you."

"That's probably true," said Bud. "Some people don't care. We don't smoke either. That's why we have them to give away."

"You are very brave," said Miller. "Most women don't want to help out with the war effort. You look like my sister. She is very beautiful."

"Thanks for the complement," replied Mary. "Can I give you a good old British hug?" Miller replied, "Sure, and I'll give you an American hug in return."

After the hugs, Mary replied, "That is the first hug I have ever been given. People don't touch me."

The remark was left unanswered and the two vehicles went on their way in opposite directions.

"Nice looking girl," said Miller. "I hope she makes it wherever she's going."

"You bet," answered Sergeant Small.

The updates to P-51s turned out to be successful and the loss rate went from 60% to 10%. The European war was over in a few months, and for the most part, the hostilities ended, even though there were a few skirmishes from time to time by axis fighter planes.

"I'm going to stop for a drink of water," said Matt.

Steve Smith stepped up and said, "I think we have run of our allotted time. Would it be possible to continue in the next meeting?"

"Thanks, Steve; I was hoping you would say that," said Matt. "I was getting I little tired."

"To the audience, thank you," said Matt.

END OF CHAPTER FOUR

CHAPTER 5

The Queen

The next breakfast of the Romeo Club was a guaranteed success. Matt had been so enjoyable the preceding Wednesday that even the waiters and cook stood in the back of the room after the meal was finished. Ashley and Maya were there, and the manager had to bring in additional tables from the storeroom. The manager announced that the food was to be at no charge and served large thick blueberry pancakes and scrambled eggs.

"Matt is so popular that I can't believe it," said Maya to Ashley. "Is this the person you are married to?"

"I knew he was good," replied Ashley, "but not this good. It kind of makes me proud. And happy. Even woman should be able to experience a day like today."

Steve Smith, the Romeo manager, rose to introduce Matt, and the crowd shouted together, "Forget the announcement, just bring on Matt!"

Matt stood up and the audience quieted down to almost complete silence.

"Good morning, everyone," said Matt. "Thanks for returning for the description of our friend the General."

"The General and I were summoned to London to solve a financial situation in the Royal Monarchy. I do not remember why we were selected, but I am honored that we were selected. When we arrived at the palace, the following announcement was posted with a green border on the palace gate: it is replica is shown on the board so you can get an idea of how well we treated.

Her Royal Highness the Queen Announces the Following Visitors to the royal monarchy:

General Les Miller, PhD, United States Army Air Force
Matthew Miller, PhD, distinguished Mathematician

The team will be assisting the Royal Family in the operation of the United Kingdom. The visit of these guests is a distinct honor to the Royal Family.

Sharply at 9:00 am, we were ushered into the Queen's office suite. She was dressed in a bright green dress with suitable jewelry. We were dressed in black suits, white shirts, and black ties. We offered a bow, and the Queen waved it off with a request that we be seated. The Queen was very sophisticated and comfortable with her position as leader of the Monarchy.

General Les Miller looked at the Queen, the Queen looked at the General, and both remarked at exactly the same time, "Do I know you?"

The Queen and the General gave each other a big American hug, and the Queen said to the General, "I can still taste that chocolate bar that you gave me on that forlorn road during the war. I was so hungry. I saved the nylons that you gave me and still have them."

The General replied, "When I saw you on that lonely road, I thought you were the prettiest girl I had ever seen. I still do."

Matt looked at the two of them in awe. Here was a Queen and a General behaving like a couple of college students. He would eventually find out, informally, that she also had a PhD that hardly anyone knew about.

The couple began to discuss their lives, since that first meeting. The queen mentioned that her father was the King and she inherited the throne. The Queen, whose nickname was 'Kitty', was busy as a representative of the people and made appearances on about 300 days in a calendar year. Management of the monarchy's finances was indeed a tedious challenge that never eased up. The General mentioned that he was a career Army officer and pilot and was certified as a fighter pilot and as a multi-engine bomber pilot. He also mentioned the fortunate events that facilitated his promotion to be a general officer.

The Queen also mentioned a downside of being Royalty. By the royal decree, no one is supposed to touch the King or Queen. For her, other than her husband who passed away recently, no person had touched her since her encounter with the General on that muddy road during the war.

The General said, "That is indeed an unfortunate circumstance, and I guarantee you that I will not abstain from giving you an occasional American hug – but not in public.

The Queen initiated the business aspects of their meeting, "Someone, we do not know who, is transferring funds from several royal accounts. We don't know who that is because there are ample funds for every royal's needs and desires. We found out about the situation from the Royal Auditor who noticed that the receiver of the transferred funds was the same numbered account. We initiated a search for the person requesting the bank transfer and it turned out to be my daughter, Princess Amelia. The Royal Auditor asked her about the bank transfer, and she indicated that it must be a mistake. She said she had not ordered any of them. There is an element of trust among royalty in that one person does not question another's integrity. I do not want to bring in the police or security services since they have a tendency to entertain the media with just about everything, resulting in a royal scandal. We would like to avoid a major scandal for any reason."

"What are the amounts of the bank transfers and how often do they occur?" asked the General.

"I can get that information for you," answered the Queen. "I also have the numbered account number right here."

"Do you have a general record of all financial transactions that occur – something like a ledger?" asked the General.

"We don't have anything like that," said the Queen. "We pay no taxes, have no driving licenses, and require no identification of any sort, such as a passport. We have no need to save information."

"It is remarkable that you have a closed society, as you have in the royalty, but in this case, it is counter-productive," said the General. "That is precisely why we have Dr. Matt Miller with us. There are methods for keeping track of any such incidents, and Matt can set it up for you."

"Well, okay then," said the Queen. "I suspect that we need something like that."

"We can and will take care of both problems. I will need access to your Royal Auditor," stated the General. "Matt will take care of the operational situation. I can guarantee to you that we will be practically transparent when we do our work. Matt will need access to the auditor and your data processing people. I think we can wrap this up in a week or 10 days."

The Queen was pleased, and the General could conceptualize a way of investigating and eliminating the bank transfer problem. Matt was awed and impressed with his grandfather, like never before.

*****

After returning to London from Zürich with the financial problem solved, the General scheduled a meeting with the Queen on Monday morning. The Queen responded immediately, confirming the appointment.

The next morning the General woke up early to another cold and dismal day. He figured they would be out of there on Wednesday. The General entered the Queen's office suite and attempted to render the necessary bow but she waved it off, as usual.

The General gave the results of the solution in Zürich, and the Queen listened politely. At the conclusion, the Queen thanked the General for a job well done and then issued a conclusion that surprised the General but gave him some insight as to how the Royalty worked.

All she said was, "I am pleased to announce that Princess Amelia has been assigned to the position of Royal Deputy to the British Ambassador in Australia. She left by private plane on Saturday night. Since I run this operation out of London and have supreme power, I made a quick decision. There will be no more surprise expenditures under my watch."

"Do you mean that you knew that Princess Amelia was the source of the problem all along?" asked the General.

"No, I did not, but I had my suspicions. The death of her ex-husband and your computer results in Zürich confirmed everything. You must remember that in the system of British Royalty, the monarch is the supreme leader."

The General responded, "I am surprised but pleased at your success."

"And now, one more thing," said the Queen. "Would you take me on a date tomorrow? I know this is common among Americans, but not for Royalty."

"I would enjoy doing that. Would you like me to make a plan for the day?" asked the General.

"I would be pleased if you did so," responded the Queen.

Bright and early the next morning – and it was a beautiful sunny day – the Queen and the General set off on their date. They both dressed in plain clothes so as not to be recognized and were driven by a chauffeur in a plain English vehicle. The first stop was Harrods, where they looked at goods on each and every floor. The Queen remarked several time, "I can hardly believe that this is how people really shop and live. It is wonderful."

The General bought the Queen a beautiful black ball pen with the name 'Harrods' printed in gold on the side. The Queen looked at the General with a twinkle in her eyes and said they were not allowed to accept gifts from English people, but the rule said nothing about Americans. The couple spent hours at Harrods, and no one recognized them.

The next stop was the bar at the Ritz hotel. An end booth was reserved so that they could gaze out at the other patrons. The Queen had an American martini, and the General had a single malt scotch. They both lingered over their drink and talked about the differences between royalty and the normal citizen. The last stop was Simpson's on the Strand, where they each had a special roast beef dinner with treacle pudding for dessert. They were both very quiet on the ride back to the palace.

The Queen said, "This was the best day of my life. Thank you." She gave the General a sophisticated kiss. "It is quite amazing that I could go for one whole day and be recognized by no one."

The day with the Queen was over."

Matt gave a big smile, and the presentation was over. In the back of the dining room were the cooks, waiters, and non-Romeo customers.

What could Steve Smith say or do. It had been the best breakfast of the Romeo Club. But he did say something. "Thank you everyone for attending. For the next meeting, we get General Miller. A pleasant good bye to all and thank you for attending."

END OF CHAPTER FIVE

CHAPTER 6

Taking a Look at Matt

At about the same time, on the next Romeo Wednesday breakfast, the General took center stage. The breakfast was 'off the menu' and the members had exactly what they wanted. As one spoken gentleman put it: "Thank goodness. No bagels and lox. I like American food." His companion said, "You got it right Joe. We get the General this week and I think he is going to be good. We are certainly fortunate to have him around. He certainly fixed this breakfast club up. We are running like clockwork." The General took center stage and got a tremendous ovation. He had no notes and stood there like he owned the restaurant.

"Good morning gentlemen and thank you for the opportunity to address you. This is my opportunity to get at Matt, who gave you an interesting picture of me. So without an adieu, here goes.

It was Sunday morning in the contiguous United States and the President and the Vice President, along with a minimal service staff, were on board the specially designed Boeing 747 airplane named Air Force One and were headed to California in a hurry. Having the President and Vice President on the same flight caused some concern with the Secret Service, who were overruled by the President. The plane headed to San Jose at the maximum speed of 700 miles per hour at 45,000 feet. The fan jet engines were running full out. The President's life-long friend and former Chief of Staff was dying and the President and that friend had made a pact to be at the others bedside if death were imminent. The friend was dying of liver disease and wasn't expected to last the day. A few hours after the President arrived, the friend passed away, and Air Force One headed back to Washington. The President always returned home to the White House every night. He never slept away from his residence except for international travel, and the First Lady always traveled with him.

When the President arrived back at the White House, it was late and he retired to a separate room in the presidential suite. He didn't want to wake the First Lady, who was nursing a bad case of the flu.

The next morning, the President awakened early to read the President Daily Brief (PDB) and learned from his aides that the First Lady was not there. The President, who was used to having everything well organized, went into a panic mode and called the Secret Service. The President also called his trusted advisors to an urgent secret meeting in the blue room of the White House. The instructions were: (1) Find the First Lady, and (2) Keep the search a total secret from everyone. No one is to know in the U.S. or in the outside world. The logic was that the Americans people would be in a panic, the stock market would take a nose dive, and the news media would turn the situation into a frenzy. Several agencies would take care of the search and not tell anyone exactly why they were doing what they were doing. The known agencies were the FBI, CIA, NSA, Police Departments, Military Intelligence, and special units from the Marines and the Army. The Chairman of the Joint Chiefs of Staff, Mark Clark, a four star general, was consulted in total secrecy. After a long day of search, there was no success.

Clark was optimistic. “We have persons in this country that operate under cover and who can solve practically any type of problem you can imagine.” Clark continued in his advice to the President, “If they are available, I’ll have them in your office in less than 12 hours.”

The President was pleased. He liked Clark. If anyone could solve the problem, then it would be Mark Clark.

General Clark called me in New Jersey on his satellite phone and caught me asleep. “Les, we have a big problem here in DC, and I’m calling to see if you and Matt are available for a short consulting job. I agreed not to mention it over the wire, but it could be the biggest problem this country has had in a while. Are you and Matt available for a pick up at 9:00 am?”

“Okay, Mark,” said the General, “We are available. Schedule a 9:00 pick up and I’ll inform Matt,” said the General. “He’s the most agreeable person on Earth, and I’m quite certain that he will agree. Maybe you don’t know it, but he thinks you are the greatest general on the Earth, and so do I. Do you know where to land here?”

“I don’t,” said Clark, “but the pilots do. I have to run to handle a crisis in international relations.”

*****

I called Matt, who had just turned on the coffee pot. I said, "Matt, something big, real big is happening, and we have been summoned to the White House. Can you be ready for a 9:00 am pickup."

"If you can be ready, then I can be ready," said Matt. "I hope you are driving."

I said I was driving and would pick him up at 8:45 at the latest.

The White House jet landed in New Jersey at 9:00 exactly and Matt and I were waiting. Both of us had a small brief case but no luggage. Matt and I knew the pilots.

"What took you so long?" I asked. "The Captain replied, "We're just slow people, General. Good morning."

"Good morning," I replied. "I suspect that you don't know what is going on."

"Not a word," said the Captain. "Jump in, we're late."

The flight was smooth and fast. Air traffic was averted for their flight, reflected in their flight plan, so the trip was as fast as they could possibly make it. A Marine One was waiting with its rotors turning. They landed at the White House heliport, and Matt and I were escorted to the President's private office.

General Clark and Kenneth L Strong, the President, were waiting, having tracked the flight of Matt and me on their electronic scoreboard.

*****

"Mr. President, I would like to introduce Matt and the General, about whom I spoke," said General Clark. "Gentlemen, this is President Strong."

"Welcome," said the President. "We have a big problem that I will describe to you. We hope you can help us with it."

I replied," We are at your service Mr. President. We don't know the problem, yet. But I assure you that if it can be solved, we can solve it."

"I hope you can," said the President.

"It will probably be straightforward, Sir," said Matt. "Please tell us, in detail, the problem, and there is a very high probability that we can take care of it in a short time."

"Well, I certainly hope you can, gentlemen. I will call in George Benson, my go-to assistant. He has been spearheading the problem so far."

The President pressed a button on his desk, and spoke the name George Benson. In a few seconds, a non-descript middle-aged gentleman was ushered in. The President said, "Gentlemen, this is George Benson. He will be in charge of the problem solution. Meanwhile, I have a scheduled meeting with the security council."

The President left through a private exit.

*****

George Benson spoke first, "My name is George Benson. The President has asked me to solve a problem of a secret nature. I have worked for him for more than twenty years."

Matt, General Clark, and I introduced ourselves to Benson.

"I will outline what we have accomplished after I delineate the problem," said Benson. It was clear that he was used to stressful situations. "The problem is that the President returned from a quick trip to California and, as the hour was late, slept in the extra bedroom in the Presidential Suite. The President returns to the White House or other residence every night that he is out of town. The First Lady had been nursing a bad case of the flu, and the President did not want to disturb her. Upon wakening early the next morning to read the President Daily Brief, the First Lady and her Secret Service escort were not in either the suite or the White House. The President always arises at 6:30 to read the PDB."

"The president instigated an alert and had an impromptu meeting with his staff," continued Benson. "He wanted his wife found, and he wanted no publicity of any kind. The secrecy is absolute. The FBI, CIA, NSA, Military Intelligence, and local Police were summoned and ordered to respond in total secrecy. A release of information would create a panic among the American people. Even the military were put on alert. You haven't heard of it because of the secrecy restriction. So far we have checked the White House thoroughly, which was a monumental task. The original architect's plans were destroyed for secrecy reasons, and there are hundreds of rooms and other places in the building. We have checked all evacuation routes and bunkers. There has been no sign of her. We have checked every means of travel including airports, train stations, automobile routes via toll stations, border patrol, hotels, and business establishments – legal and illegal. All of this was performed in total secrecy. The President thinks it might be a form of kidnapping, even though the FBI has said there is no evidence of that. There is no avenue that we have not explored. We have even checked the tunnel from the White House to the bunker beneath the Treasury Building. They came up with nothing there. Now the President is concerned about foreign adversaries, so the President has said we will have to go public fairly soon if she is not located."

"We can solve your problem," said Matt. "We will use a technique known as *Reverse Mathematics* that applies to problems of this type."

"We will use it on your problem," said Matt. "Here is how we should approach the problem of the First Lady. Your team from the FBI, CIA, and so forth, as good as they are, are going after the First Lady by looking in places she could be. They should be looking where she shouldn't or wouldn't be. So the question is, what are the places where she shouldn't be, and I guarantee there will not be too many of them around. So I would like a tour, together with the General, of the total scene of investigation."

George Benson had a look on his face that read, 'Is this guy for real?' So they started on a tour of the entire scene, not a crime scene, since no crime had been committed. The group toured every office in the White House and checked all of the private exits. They looked at the attic and all of the secret little rooms that are too small to be recognized ordinarily. The White House architect, many years earlier, had recorded none of his plans, nor did the builder, who didn't seem use any plans at all. Some say it was for security. They toured the bunker at the Treasury Building and the tunnel leading there from the White House. The tunnel was constructed during World War II and was totally deserted. Along the way were many closed and locked rooms labeled 'Cot Room # xx, for use by support people in the event of an attack. The rooms probably hadn't been opened since they were constructed and were stocked with bottled water and k-rations in the 1940s. There were no keys to the rooms, since they never had been used. Matt said to Benson in a sharp tone he rarely used. "You should get the Army Corps of Engineers in here and open the doors. Got it?"

Benson, not used to such authoritative talk, did just that. It is amazing how quickly the Army Corps of Engineers can respond. In an hour, the first door was opened. Nothing. So they asked Matt what to do, and he responded as if they were a bunch of children, "Look at the handles. They are covered with 50 years of dust and dirt."

The engineers did as ordered and discovered one with no dust or dirt. They opened that door, and voila! There was the First Lady and the Secret Service agent.

Matt said, "Give me a few minutes with them." He was as cool as a cucumber.

If you have never seen Dr. Matt Miller, you should know that he is tall, slender, deeply tanned from golfing, and he speaks with a calm reassuring tone that makes a person respect him.

"We've been looking for you," said Matt. "A few people were getting worried. How did you get in here?"

"I had a key from World War II in the 1940s," replied the Secret Service agent. "Several of us were stationed here. I know I don't look that old, but I am."

"Next, Ma'am, why are you here?" asked Matt. "I won't tell anyone. It's only between you and me. But, don't worry. I'll fix things up for you."

"I just have this awful flu and look at me," said the First Lady. "I look like a witch. I'm blubbering all over the place. I've been crying, and my hair is a total mess."

Matt said to the Secret Service agent, "Why did you do it?" "Because she asked me to. That's my job," was the answer. "I have to do what she asks or tells me to do."

Matt came out of the cot room, and asked Benson to call the President. "Tell him that the First Lady has been found and to come to cot room #37 with her raincoat and a rain hat. Pronto!"

The President arrived in less than 10 minutes, and Matt said, "Be kind to her, Mr. President, she needs you now."

Matt and the General met with the President in his private office. "Thank you, gentlemen," said the President. "You've solved my crisis, and I will be eternally grateful. Please send me a bill for whatever amount you please."

"There is no need Mr. President," I said. "Our work is gratis."

On the way home in the White House jet, both Matt and I were very pleased. Matt said, "That certainly was a worthwhile trip."

"It was indeed," I said.

"I could use a good round of golf," said Matt. "Sounds good to me," I answered.

"Life is good."

And that is the end of the story. Thank you."

Matt just sat there without moving. Finally he said quietly, "Thank you very much Sir."

The cooks, waiters, and guests were in the back of the room listening. One of them started clapping and the whole room picked up on it. It was a very successful meeting.

"One more thing," said Steve Smith. "For those of you who would like to help us out with an interesting story, please call me before the next meeting. To all of you, thank you for attending. It was fun."

END OF CHAPTER SIX

CHAPTER 7

The Source

Charles Johnson called Steve Smith, the Romeo Club's leader. "Steve, this is Charles. How are you doing?"

"Not bad," said Smith. "I was just thinking about the program for the next Romeo breakfast. Matt and the General, as speakers are hard to beat. As a retired government employee, do you have any ideas?"

"I do, and that is the reason I called. There is a ton of information in the country's archive and there are more than a few descriptions of the episodes of Matt and the General. So, I called Matt at his university and he was more than cordial. He is a real gentleman in addition to being a scholar. I posed a hypothetical. If we used one of the Matt, Ashley, and the General's episodes for the Romeo Club, would there any problem using the trio's first and last names. He said the information was in the public domain, and we were free to use all of the information, as well as their names. So here is what I can do for you. Select some episodes and paraphrase them and turn them over to you. You can then select a member to present them. I would prefer to be a hidden source. Is that okay?"

"I can hardly believe you, Charles, and all I can say is 'yes' and 'thank you'," replied Smith. "How much lead time do you need?"

"What you don't know is that I am professional writer and can knock off a half dozen or so in a week and at the latest 10 days," said Charles. "They will not be in any chronological order. I am looking at one now that took place during the pandemic."

"One last question," asked Smith. "Do I have to notify the team before making the presentation at one of our breakfasts?"

"Matt said no," said Charles. "You may do what you want to do and when you want to do it. I have to cut this conversation off; there is someone at the door. We are getting a new walk-in bathing facility."

*****

Smith called Richard Evans, a previous speaker, and asked if he would like to give another presentation. Since he liked his previous but short presentation. All Evan said was he would be pleased to do it, but said he might need to use a few speaking notes. Smith replied that would be no problem. He would receive the gist of the presentation forthwith.

END OF CHAPTER SEVEN

CHAPTER 8

The Rescue

Richard Evans arrived at the next Romeo Club breakfast in a long-sleeved shirt, a tie, and a fashionable sport coat. Several men asked why and he just said they would find out later. The word spread around and the men ate their breakfast in no time. That's the way men are. They respond innately to a situation.

"Good morning gentleman and any ladies that might be present. I will be the speaker this fine morning and I have an interesting program for you. It is an international intrigue.

So buckle your seat belts for an enjoyable journey.

Mark Clark, Director of Intelligence, contacted the team of Matt, Ashley and the General concerning an international problem that had arisen in England. The Queen's son Prince Michael and his son, the Prince of Bordeaux, with the regal name Prince Philip George William Charles were missing. Prince Michael was an internationally known scientist with a PhD in astrophysics from Oxford, and was instrumental in developing a vaccine for the COVID pandemic. The reason for the kidnapping was not known and also where he was being held. Using diplomatic channels, the United States was contacted who employed a complicated network of informants and believed it was Iran. The major concern was that Iran was developing a nuclear weapon and they needed assistance on their project. The objective was to extract the Prince and his son out of Iran to a friendly country.

Then Intelligence developed a plan to use an Iranian spy turned to favor the Americans to locate the Prince and his son and use American personnel to perform the extraction. The Iranian spy, named Atalus, or Adam Benfield in the American domain, was selected to locate the son and the Prince and assist an American team that would perform the extraction. The Iranians kept the Prince and his son separate so an extraction would not be attempted, believing that the Prince would never leave without his son. The team of Dr. Matt Miller, Ashley Miller, and Dr. Les Miller, known as the General, were selected to perform the complicated task.

The plan was to have the team go to Iran, locate the Prince and the son, and have Adam Benfield drive them at an opportune time to a deserted airfield to be picked up and transported to the neighboring country of Israel. Details of the operation were the responsibility of Matt, Ashley, and the General. The two main elements of their plan was to get the team into Iran and how to get themselves and the abducted victims safely out.

The operational part of the plan was to be developed by Matt and executed and managed by Ashley and the General.

The exit vehicle was designed by Matt and the General as a modified drone to carry passengers, since drones were not considered to be a threat by the Iranians. It was to be developed by the military's prime contractor as a pair of vehicles, one being a decoy. Matt, Ashley, and the General were to attend governmental foreign language school to learn Farsi. The courses consisted of two-week total immersion followed by a one week of the methodology of covert operations and social interactions.

The drones were modified to take land and off from a grassy plain. The Iranian Sukhoi air field was deserted and could be used. Iran had ordered a fleet of Sukhoi fighter planes from Russia, and Iran built a special field for them. Then Iran experienced a budget problem, because the U.S. blocked their bank funds and the order was cancelled. The field – the runways and buildings – are unused and totally accessible.

Russian passports for Ashley, her male escort, Matt, and the General were obtained through the English Monarchy. Ashley and her escort would enter Iran through conventual airlines since Ashley would be dressed like an Iranian woman. Meanwhile, Matt and the General would fly to the Drone Base in Israel. The drones will have been transported to the Drone Base in C-17 transport planes.

On the day of the operation, Ashley will fly to Tehran by an accomplish of Benfield's and Matt and the General will be transported to the Sukhoi air field by the drone. Benfield will pick them up and go to an expensive hotel. Ashley will become acquainted with little Prince Philip.

As an interesting sidelight, the General was more calm about the Iranian mission than he would normally be the case. Matt asked why, and the General was more that pleased to tell him that he had met two Iranian students when he was getting his MS degree in computer science in New York. The Iranians loved American life, especially beer, hamburgers, and American women. The President of the university was a financial consultant to the Shah of Iran and the two students were part of the deal. The two men were excellent students and one of them was even translating the professor's computer book to Farsi.

On the day of the penetration of Iran by the drone, the U.S. military planned for the mission and had an F-117 fighter based on an aircraft carrier as an escort. The American fighter plane was invisible to radar. Nothing occurred and the F-117 returned to the ship without incident.

The operation was planned on a religious weekend in Iran. Matt and the General were escorted by Benfield in a Mercedes S500 sedan to the meeting room. The Iranians are rich people if you are in the right group. No one paid any attention to Matt and the General to their first meeting, and they got to use their knowledge of the Farsi language. In about 15 minutes, Prince Michael entered with two body guards and started to lecture in English. The audience seemed to understand English. The Prince's lecture on viral science was well prepared and very technical; it was not clear that the audience understood what was going on. Matt made eye-contact with Prince Michael, who recognized Matt and flicked his eye. Prince Michael and Matt knew each other.

The next morning, Benfield repeated his trip to the Biology building with Matt and the General. After about an hour, Matt and the General were approached by a tall Iranian officer. "Excuse me, do I know you?" he said to the General. "Did we attend the university together?"

The General looked at the officer and said, "Yes you do. We were in the same master's class together. You were from Iran, and your name is ..". The General thought for a few seconds and said, "you are Robert Peterson, and your associate student was John Evans, and you were both from Iran. "

"That's true," said Robert Peterson. "You have a good memory. My Iran name is different. I am the country's technology officer, equivalent to an American Vice President. I would like to talk to you."

Our cover has been blown, thought Matt. I wonder about this guy Benfield. We are in big trouble. Real big trouble. I'm going to have to figure out a way to get us out of this situation. The four men were escorted by a guard to a separate room.

The Iranian technology officer initiated the conversation. "My American studies enabled me to attain my high position. I can have you put in prison or even executed." The General swallowed and cleared his throat. Matt looked into his eyes and he saw fear.

"We are here to extract Prince Michael," said Matt.

"I know," said Peterson. "I had it done."

"Why didn't you ask him to be a consultant to your country?" asked Matt.

"That is not the way things are done in Iran," said Peterson. "I have no control over that."

"I have a PhD in mathematics from a university in California," continued Peterson. "I know of you. You are a mathematics scholar. You are Matt Miller." Matt thought to himself that a bond had been made between the two men. His brain was working in high gear.

"Why did you do this?" asked the General.

"Our country is dying from then COVID virus, as you call it, and no country will provide us with a vaccine. We can pay for it," said Peterson. The General was totally flustered. Matt was as cool as a cucumber. "Can we make a deal?" asked Matt.

"All options are open," answered Peterson.

"Can you exchange the four of us – the General, your friend Atalus, Prince Michael, and me for a working vaccine for all of your country," asked Matt.

"I can do anything," said Peterson. "I have the power to release you as soon as you guarantee the vaccine."

I can give you an answer in minutes," replied Matt. "If you will direct me to an outdoors area where I can make a satellite call to the U.S."

Matt called Kimberly Scott, a government associate in Washington on his wrist satellite phone. Kimberly understood the plan is seconds.

"We have plenty of vaccine" she said. "Let me call President Strong."

Kimberly responded in 5 minutes. "He will guarantee the vaccine free of charge to Iran if England will guarantee a minimal amount. Here are the figures. Iran has 80 million people. 60 million are adults. We will guarantee 40 million doses if England will guarantee 20 million. As a side comment, he will guarantee all 60 million, if necessary. He said England should give a little. After all, the guy Michael is from England. I have to call the General's old buddy Sir Bunday and he can contact the prime minister. Just give me a few minutes. Hold on."

"I have a response already," Kimberly said. "England will guarantee 20 million doses. The following is important to complete the transaction. We expect to transfer the vaccine in refrigerated trucks loaded into C-17s. We can load our 40 million doses into two refrigerated trucks in one C-17, and England can load their 20 million doses into one C-17, along with a truck. The three trucks in two C-17s will be delivered to Iran at Sukhoi air field in one week – probably 5 days. Iran has to guarantee they will do diligence and provide sufficient medical staff to handle the doses pf vaccine. We will provide two doctors and one nurse to train them. Who is your contact in Iran?

"Dr. Robert Peterson," said Matt. "He is VP of technology for the entire country and educated in the states." "Okay," said Kimberly. "We have him in our database. By the way, this Sir Charles Bunday, known as Buzz, is a wonder. I asked him how much he is getting for his work. He said $3 million and I raised it to $4 million."

"You are a nice person and a genius," said Matt. "I know," said Kimberly, "just doing my job. I hope to meet you some day.

Matt relayed the news to Robert Peterson, the General, and Benfield. Peterson was pleased beyond belief.

At noon of the first day of the holy season, Ashley and little Prince Philip were transported in an armor-plated Mercedes S500 to Sukhoi air field. At approximately the same time, Prince Michael, the General, Matt, and Benfield were being transported in a similar car to Sukhoi air field. The twin drones arrived at the scheduled time and the group was flown to the Drone Base in Israel. The mission was over and no one seemed to notice that Adam Benfield might lose his cover and would forever be a target of Iranian security police. But Peterson was pleased so you never know what he would do. Everyone was transferred to London in the General's Gulfstream 650 and disbursed from there.

Richard Evans, the speaker, was tired and as usual, the rear of the restaurant was filled with employees, visitors, and also

Ashley and Maya. What about Matt and the General? They were there too.

*****

Smith called Jim Hefner, a previous speaker, and asked if he would like to give another presentation. His previous presentation was thoroughly enjoyed. All Hefner said was he would be pleased to do it, but said he might need to use a few speaking notes. Smith replied that would be no problem. Hefner would receive the gist of the subject forthwith.

END OF CHAPTER EIGHT

CHAPTER 9

The Escape

Jim Hefner arrived at the Romeo breakfast dressed in his usual washable trousers and a blue polo shirt. He looked ready for golf, which he probably was. He stood up with an enormous smile and said, "Here I am again. You must have liked my first presentation. This talk has an international flavor to it. It could have happened in actual life so pretend it is real. So let's get started

"The team of Matt, Ashley, and the General had just finished with the rescue operation from Iran and needed a rest. The President had said there was another issue just around the corner, but the team could take a vacation at the governments expense. The team selected Hawaii; the men played golf, since Hawaii had more challenging golf courses than any other state in the union. The women worked on their suntan. They all took advantage of good Hawaiian food. As always, it had to end, as it always does.

This issue involves the country of China and the effort could have been named The Chinese Problem. All the U.S. needed to know was to find out what China was doing in the area of space technology and hyper speed aircraft. While we are at it, it could be useful to send over some disinformation. The General asked the Director of National Intelligence, Mark Clark, and is wife Ann, previously an Army combat offer, to accompany them. While enjoying their work on her sun tan, Ann asked Ashley about the next project. After Ashley replied, Ann noted that something was wrong. Usually, politicians tell you the information they want beforehand, and it is your job to get it and tell how you got it. It looked like this was to be a different kind of project.

While relaxing in Maui, Matt called his contact in Washington, Kimberly Scott, the top-notch information analyst, about what the U.S. military was doing in space technology. After a little searching on the nation's super computer, Kimberly responded the it was the V-35 space plane. The project is not secret but what it can do was secret. Kimberly continued that the Chinese probably heard of the nation's space vehicle, military drone, high speed fighter, space supply ship, and booster – all in one. The Chinese were probably having fits, and lied that they were doing essentially the same thing. But what, Matt asked himself, were they really doing.

Matt remarked that needed to get someone with access to the Chinese military that could provide what they are actual doing. Matt knew from his mathematical studies that the Chinese are quite interested in mathematics and historically sent visiting professors all over the world. In their mind, it was better than doing it yourself. Matt immediately called his PhD friend Harp Thomas that was teaching math at the main Swiss university to find out if there were any Chinese math professors in sabbatical in Switzerland. Harp mentioned that he had a climbing buddy named Wuan Singh, a former defense worker, who had been approached by his government to consider spying on the U.S. Apparently, his father lives in the states. I'll mention it to him on our next climb that is this coming weekend.

Harp returned from the climb with news for Matt. The Chinese government wants Singh to figure out a way of spying on the U.S. government. They have money and will support any idea he might have. We could run him as a double agent said Matt. We could supply him with false information and he could inform us with information in what the Chinese are doing in the 'space war'. We would even give him a U.S. source; one that doesn't actually exist. We could ask Kimberly to get us a *nonper* at a hypothetical location.

What is a *nonpeer*, asked Harp. Matt answered, it is a name for a person that doesn't exist. We could even add a university to go along with it. I'll get some false information to supply his Chinese supporters, if you will give it to him. We could let the project roll and see what happens. We could even guarantee a U.S. citizenship if his cover is blown in the process.

Matt contacted Kimberly Scott again and she knew exactly what he required in the way of information. Two hours later Kimberly sent the following bogus information to Matt via satellite phone:

> *The U.S. position on space*: The U.S. military is getting out of space because of Global warning.

> *The preparation*: The U.S. has built an underwater military vehicle named a **Subcraft** along with underwater buildings and underwater military housing. Underwater bombs are under research. In fact, the U.S. has been test underwater bombs in the Atlantic Ocean and the Pacific Ocean and that is the cause of the

worldwide bad weather. A fictitious date for the fictitious plan was given as 5 years.

The Chief Person in Charge and information source: A *nonpeer* by the name of Dr. Alan Taylor, a professor at B.I.T (Boston Institute of Technology).

The U.S. mole currently in China: Dr. George Redmark.

Dr. Redmark will contact Singh. Singh should give the Chinese information to Redmark who will forward it to this country via secret channels. If the operation is discovered, Redmark will have an escape route for Singh and himself.

Harp delivered the information to Wuan Singh at the James Joyce pub in Zürich and Singh replied that China would supply the air fare and a generous stipend for him. Matt told harp that Singh would be given $1 million and guaranteed U.S. protection, and he, Harp Thomas would receive an honorarium of $4 million via direct deposit for his efforts. Harp thought it seemed a bit high, but Matt remarked it was a line in a secret budget.

Once Matt heard of the *nonpeer* Alan Taylor, he asked if the name were anonymous and Kimberly sheepishly said they never thought of checking it out. At that point it was too late.

Matt and Ashley returned to the states to let operation happen at it's own speed. In two days, Redmark informed U.S. Intelligence that the Chinese claims concerning their space warfare was bogus. Redmark also mentioned that Singh had supplied the bogus U.S. information about subcraft to the Chinese military, and it was accepted and applauded. Singh had been given first class lodging in an expensive hotel. In the third evening, Redmark approached Singh that they had to get out before morning. Someone had check the *nonper* at B.I.T. and a person with that name actually existed the mole had planned for all conditions. He had a Yak-152 plane, formerly used as a Russian military aircraft but now was sport plane, and they would have to take it across the Bering Sea to an unused military airport in Russia named the Folding Airport. But did not know what to do from there.

Matt again sprung into action. He had a math colleague from Russia whose father owned a Yak-152 sport plane who agreed to take Redmark and Singh from Folding Airport near the sea to an unused military Russian airport just north of Moscow for $1 million. The deal was consummated and the transportation was enabled. They were met by a military plane that offered transportation to the states. Redmark took advantage of it. Singh wanted to go back to Switzerland because he felt his position was secure.

As usual, the General ended the mission with, "case closed."

"And that, ladies, gentlemen, and visitors is the end of my contribution to the Romeo Club, and I am ready for a round of golf," said Jeff Hefner.

Jeff Hefner got an enormous round of applause."

*****

Smith called George Short, who had participated before and had a pleasing personality, and asked if he would like to give another presentation. His previous presentations were thoroughly enjoyed and Smith was sure George could do as well or better. All Short said was he would be pleased to do it, but said he might need to use a few speaking notes. Smith replied that would be no problem. Short would receive the gist of the subject forthwith from Smith.

END OF CHAPTER NINE

Chapter 10

The Royal Baby

Steve Smith introduced George Short who stood up and looked a bit uncomfortable. Smith noticed it and said, "I would like to tell about something that happened to me that gives me a chuckle every time I think of it. I was working in Switzerland and my wife and I invited my manager for dinner at our apartment. Now it should be realized that the Swiss are devoted to wine, perhaps not as much as the French, but almost as much. My wife went to the Migros market there and purchased the preparations. I had asked her to get some wine but not some crummy stuff. She did. During dinner, my manager said the wine was excellent and asked about it. I said I did not know much about wine but my wife always bought on price. He and his wife were impressed. Afterwards, I said to her, "What kind of wine was that you bought?" Her answer was that she did not know what to do and didn't want to waste money so she bought the cheapest wine in the whole store. The audience laughed and the ice was broken and George Short started in.

George Short cleared his throat and started in. He was nervous but after about 10 words, he was back to normal. He had a pleasing voice and the audience just settled back in their chairs. He started out by saying that he was an actuary and worked with numbers and mathematics for the duration of his career. He worked up to being the chief actuary at the world's biggest insurance company. He had taken a course at the Toastmaster's Club when he first started out after college and it helped him some but he wasn't exactly good at it. Jeff Hefner, the speaker at the last Romeo Club meeting, said, "George, you sound perfect to me." Everyone agreed and George was off and running – as they say.

It seems as though the story centers around Matt, Ashley, and the General, as introduced previously, but not that much. Matt's friend at the university had aspirations to become an actress, knowing at the start that advancement would be difficult. She started out in the New York scene and did a lot of work in restaurants as a waitress. She finally made into the TV industry and developed into a bone fide TV star and attracted a Prince in the English Royal Monarchy.

From day one, the English media and the paparazzi were against her for two reasons: she wasn't English and she was bi-racial, or rather, she thought so, and they thought she was bi-racial also. They were married in a glorious ceremony, but from the first day of their marriage, she was treated with disrespect. She had no privacy and had no control of her life. Then Queen gave them a luxurious home to live in and she had all the money to live like a future Queen. Royalty must have children and before long she was childbearing, and the paparazzi went to work on her full speed. At least the paparazzi and the media thought she was childbearing.

The princess called Matt in the United States; she did not want to be a mother and Matt and the General went to work.

They used their knowledge of the government scene and attracted a surrogate mother for the princess. Meanwhile, the paparazzi and the media centered around the size of her stomach and noticed it grew and noted that it must be a pad. As the size of her stomach grew, they wrote that she just increased the size of the pad. The mother of the surrogate baby was approached concerning a possible role as a U.S. spy in England, which she turned down, However, she agreed to take on the role as a nanny of the surrogate baby. Her name was Emma Williams.

At just about the time that the royal baby was to have her baby, the surrogate mother gave birth in the states and the surrogate baby was transported to London in a secret airplane and transported to Penelope the Prince's wife. The baby was born and no one knew if the baby was a real baby or a surrogate baby. The paparazzi and the media went wild and made Penelope's life miserable. However, the mother of the surrogate baby served as the nanny to her very own baby. She loved the position. For her, it was a good deal. The queen was a tricky old person and got the information about the spy business out of the nanny, even though that option was never exercised.

On a Saturday on her day off, the nanny looked the wrong way as she was crossing Charing Cross Road in London and was killed. To this day, the English people do not know if the baby is a real baby of Penelope or a surrogate.

Back in the states afterwards, Matt got a saliva test from a Starbucks coffee cup and had an academic associate do a DNA test on Penelope's sample. Penelope was not biracial. Her parents were biracial, she was adopted, and they raised her to be biracial for social reasons.

Penelope and the Prince are still married and are a dazzling couple. But to this day, they do get excessive bad press from the media.

Well, that's it for me said George Short. I love the story but would like to know the details of what really happened.

George was a success and as usual, the rear of the breakfast room was filled with employees and other customers.

*****

Steve Smith asked George Short if he would like to do another presentation and Short agreed to do it. The subject would be The Royal Marriage. In this case, Short would be short.

END OF CHAPTER TEN

CHAPTER 11

The Royal Marriage

You would think that having given a talk two weeks ago and having a successful career would assist a person about being nervous before speaking to a crowd. Then, George was a different kind of guy. Steve Smith sensed it again, and started off the day's entertainment. "I have another story about my Swiss manager. A few months after I left Switzerland, he and his family visited the U.S. and came to visit with us for 3 or 4 days. They brought us a bottle of special alcohol to drink. I do not know if it was whisky or what it was, but it was alcohol, for sure. I'm not an alcohol drinker. I drank a bit of wine in Switzerland – well actually more just a bit – and I always said that when I got home, that was it for the drinking. It is so. I haven't touched a drop, although I believe a person should do what they want to do. The bottle they brought had a pear in it. I figured it out on the spot, but he insisted on telling me about it. When the pear was just a bud, they put a bottle around it and cut it off when the pear was fully developed. They filled the bottle with alcohol and put a cap on it. If you drink the alcohol, you can just fill the bottle again and the pear will be preserved. Before that, a graduate assistant to whom I was nice gave me a present that consisted of an unopened bottle of Chivas Regal, an expensive whisky. It hasn't been touched either in more than 30 years. George loosened up and Smith introduced him and mentioned the subject would be about a happy royal marriage – well maybe not so happy.

Good morning," said George Short. "I have another interesting story about the royal people. It is about marriage. Remember when we left off, Emma had died. A few people were worried, and in particular the General and his Army buddy and wing man, Sir Charles "Buzz" Bunday who was in the British Security Services (BSS). Could it be that the Monarchy was in the process of cleaning house. As time passed, the concern grew and the surveillance of the Duchess – what Penelope was referred to as – increased. When she was being watched, she did absolutely nothing. The General and "Buzz" got worried enough and planned an extraction. Moreover, the Monarchy had taken the Duchess' U.S. passport. How could they get her out of the United Kingdom and back to the States.

The Duchess and the Duke, that was what Michael was referred to as, had a happy marriage. They were nice to one another. The Duke even gave her a new personal Jaguar automobile for her pleasure. But as she drove around London, she was constantly followed. Buzz, the General, and Matt decided to use that to their advantage for the extraction. Here was the plan they drummed up. It had been used by the BSS before. The basic idea involved a fake suicide, an Army outfit, and an extraction as an Army person. London has cameras on all streets except behind the Scotland Yard building that had the windows blackened for security. The Duchess would drive behind the Scotland Yard building and stop with the engine running and get out of the car. A BSS frogman would direct the

Duchess to a black car right behind them. He would drive her car, the Jaguar, to the center of the London Bridge, and jump in to the Thames River. He would swim to the shore and disappear. The Duchess would enter the black car and be driven to a safe house. The Duchess and the frogman would wear the same-colored clothes so bystanders would think the frogman was the Duchess. To prevent the car following the Duchess to see what was going on, the BSS would stage an automobile accident. At the safe house, Matt dressed in an Army uniform as a Lieutenant Colonel would give the Duchess an Army uniform dressed as a Captain. At the request of a General officer, that is our General, the U.S. military would prepare the needed uniforms and needed additional things, such as shoes and undergarments, for Penelope as well as a new passport for her. They would leave from the London city Airport and land at a secret airbase in New Hampshire, from which the crew will be brought to the General's home in New Jersey and the extraction was complete and Penelope was saved.

Back in London, Penelope's body never showed up and the Queen settled on a body that turned up without an autopsy. Things settled down in the Monarchy and Prince Michael would go on to earn a PhD in Astrophysics and become a scientist of note.

In the U.S., Penelope was given a full-face lift and a new Name, passport, and driver's license. She was now Sara Nicole Harris and given a good position in the General's company in upper New York. The title was Vice President. The new Sara was given a new home worth $300,000, a yearly salary of $200,000, and a new car. However, the new Sara truly loved Michael. They did everything together, but now things had changed.

Sara joined the company and at first, the results looked promising. However, her application of the new technology and her interactions with other members were not satisfactory. She was fired by the General. The new Sara then returned to England.

Sara Nicole Harris ran into Michael at a polo match. He did not immediately know that the women he approached was his previous Duchess. And that is the end of a happy marriage.

*****

Steve Smith asked George Short if he would like to do another presentation and Short agreed to do it. The subject would be The General and Royal Family. In this case, Short would not be really short because it is a long subject; the General has had a long and interesting career.

END OF CHAPTER ELEVEN

Chapter 12

The General and Royal Family

Steve Smith introduced George Short who seemed right at home in front of an audience. He smiled and talked to a friend in the first row of tables. Someone in the back yelled, "What happened George, did you take a slug of whisky." Someone else said, "That's not George, you're looking at an imposter." George just smiled and said, "It's all because you are a fine audience." Steve Smith said, "Well then, let's get going. By the way, the real General is here. Welcome General and his buddy Matt and of course, Ashley and her friend Maya."

"We are back to the General again, and I mean the General in this room," said George. "It's all from the national archive with his permission and also his associates. There is nothing negative, and in general, it is most spectacular. I will be talking in the first person, as though I am telling a story, which indeed it is."

As a young boy, Les Miller was interested in the dynamics of flight and earned his pilot's license as a teenager. In college he was a good student and majored in math and minored in international relations. He entered the Army – there was no Air Force at that time – with the promise of a chance at pilot training. If he couldn't be a pilot he could be a navigator because of his excellent math background. He graduated from college as a 2nd Lieutenant and his pilot training helped him get a chance at single engine training or multi-engine training, referring to fighter planes and bomber planes, respectively. He selected single engine training with the request that he could go into multi-engine training after his first tour of duty was completed. What Les did not realize was that fighter pilots had a 60% chance of being shot down or captured. Les completed military pilot training as a 1st Lieutenant and completed his combat tour of duty of 25 missions and was promoted to being a Captain in the Army Air force. Les flew with a wing man named Charles "Buss" Bunday who would become a lifetime friend and associate in many interesting instances.

After being promoted to Captain, Les participate in a secret project for armor plating P-51 fighters that reduced the casualty rate to 10%, after which he was promoted to Lieutenant colonel for a genuine contribution to World War Two. Colonel Miller, which he then was, participated in the famous Doolitle raid on Japan that turned the war in the Pacific around in favor of the allies. Actually, the history of the Dootlitle raid is a little sketchy and that might be exactly true. Subsequently, Colonel Miller participated in the 1000 plane bombing of Berlin that effectively ended World War II in Europe. Colonel Miller was a serious fellow and neither smoked or drank alcohol, but enjoyed various tours when on leave, such as lecturing to the graduating students at West Point. However, one of the most noteworthy achievements occurred when a large transport was flying a Four-Star General, Colonel Miller, some lower-level officers, and a lot of soldiers from Germany to the states. In route, a German fighter pilot did not believe that the war was over, and shot and killed the Captain and First Officer to the transport plane. The military people on the transport plane were terrified – especially the General. Lieutenant Colonel saved the day by landing the plane in Labrador for which he was promoted to full Colonel.

Promotions were few and far between after the wars were over, and Colonel Miller was stuck without promotion until an older officer retired. Miller used this time to earn a PhD in International Relations, an MS in computer Science, and work in the OSS. Colonel Miller was subsequently promoted to be a General officer and he is what we have here today.

The General used his knowledge to form a substantial political polling company and uses his profits to help people.

One of his most successful projects in that domain was his work for the English Monarchy. He and Matt worked with the monarchy to solve a financial problem and introduce block chain technology into the royalty.

One last thing. I have been advised that the General, Matt, and Ashley have worked on several important projects that are covered in subsequent breakfast meetings.

"Thank you."

"George Short, you are a wonder," said Steve Smith. "You have made a lifetime of important work into an interesting summary. Everyone, let's have a big round of applause."

*****

Steve was in a quandary. Should he get into the COVID pandemic or not. So, he asked Matt, who he could count on giving a thoughtful and professional answer. Mat said, "Steve, thanks for asking me for my opinion. I would say yes and think we should start with the virus itself that many people honestly tried to forget about. If it ever happens again, we should know more about what we should do."

"Matt, would you do it?" asked Steve. "It's a touchy subject."

"I would be honored to do it," answered Matt., "We have an extra week in-between, and I could probably use it. Thanks for a good series of breakfast meetings."

END OF CHAPTER TWELVE

CHAPTER 13

The Virus

Matt and the General were approached unannounced by two men from the government and were asked if they would be willing to take on a secret project that could effect the United States and possibly the rest of the world. There was evidence – or perhaps a fear – that the COVID was being used as a bioweapon against the country and other countries, as well. The project had a large budget and world be approached as a project one operation, meaning that it was the nations leading project. The total project was to be kept secret but the persons involved could be from foreign countries. The project had a secret line item in the annual budget and would be financed for one year. Afterwards, the results would be evaluated and the project concluded or extended. The work was in the domain of a team led by the General as the manger, and Mat as the chief technical resource. Matt and the General accepted the positions forthwith.

The first activity was to form the team and the General with the help of Matt immediately identified key resources they had worked with previously. They are:

The General
Matt
Dr. Purgoine (known as Anna)
Ashley
Charles (Buzz) Bunday
William Bunday
Harp Thomas
Kimberly Jobsen Thomas
Gustav Snider
Harry Steevens
Amelia Robinson

The first operation of the team was to gather relevant information about the cause, event, or group of persons that caused the pandemic. After all, you can't find a solution without a cause. Here is Matts list:

- China wanted to dominate and economic and military power of the world.
- A formerly successful company wanted to reset then economic system to be again successful.
- A middle eastern group or country with the intention of destroying America.
- An internal agency of a major country reset America for political reasons.
- An unrecognized force of nature.
- An individual scientist.
- A satellite system with unknown capability.
- A result of a space launch.
- Something from outer space

The General agreed it was a good way to start, but did not know exactly how to go about getting a solution. Matt suggested they put Ashley and Anna to work on searching the Internet for relevant ideas. This was Anna's first cut at the problem:

- What kind of virus was it and how was it identified.
- What is its source.
- Where was it most prevalent.
- How was it transmitted.
- What are the symptoms.
- How is it diagnosed.
- How long does it last after diagnosis?
- What is the medical group doing.
- Who is leading the treatment.

Ashley wondered where Anna came up with the ideas, and she mentioned that she had lived through the polio epidemic of the 1950s.

Ashley got to work on the known history of what was going on and came up with a lengthy history. It was quite long and here is a simple snapshot:

"It is generally felt the virus known a COVID-19 first entered the country on a flight China to LAX airport in mid-March of the year 2020. The flight was far from full with 49 passengers and 8 crew members. In the 6-hour trip, the passenger shared restrooms, cabin air, and a narrow aisle. A retired surgeon in first class was infected with the virus, that he had contracted in January in Wuhan, China and thoroughly disrupted the entire country of China, even though it was centered in Wuhan. How and why the virus spread in the U.S. so rapidly is unknown."

The history is extensive and is worth reading and much to long for this presentation. But is available in the project description in the archives However the quest for information was started, and the team could move on from there.

After some time and much analysis, it became known that a definite answer would never be completely known. There surfaced several options and they had to be rated, so an arbitrary scale was formulated. Here are the elements of that scale are as following range:

Rarely | unlikely | probably | most-likely | without-a-doubt | for-sure.

Then the options could be combined and an answer to the open question could be formulated. This was relevant analytics at that time, and the best the team could do. Through some complicated analysis the following conclusion was drawn by the team:

Natural source – 0.72 (72%}
Man-made – 0.28 (28%)
Alternate source – 0.00 (0%)

Through the total study, no bioweapon became evident.

As a final remark, this is a complicated but very interesting problem. The pandemic is over, but its lingering head is likely to arise in the future. We are fortunate to have leading scientists working on it.

Thanks for listening.

A fellow in the back of the room said, “That was more than excellent Matt. It will be a very long before will have a presentation as excellent.” The audience clapped more loudly and long than ever before.

****

Steve Smith took the stage once again. The audience was somber. It was a serious subject.

“In two weeks, we will have presentation on the Pandemic. I hope we will see you all again.”

END OF CHAPTER THIRTEEN

CHAPTER 14

The Pandemic

Steve Smith introduced Daniel Robertson, a long time Romeo member that was still working when he was still working, at least that is the way that Daniel phrased it. He intended on spending the requisite time preparing for the presentation but was called away when a plane crashed in Australia. He made notes on the flight to Australia and on the way back, and that's about it. Daniel has spoken many times before the group and Steve was confident that he would be more than comfortable with a talk on the pandemic.

"Good morning," said Daniel Robertson. "I'm going to talk to you about the pandemic this morning, but I am sorry to say that something happened and I was called away. On the flight to Australia, I made a ton of notes, but I did not have time to put them all together in a meaningful whole. So anyway, here goes and hope for the best."

"A lone woman is transported to Washington, DC by a fast jet, manufactured by a large aerospace company. The woman is driven quickly to the President's private office. The story begins at this point.

The woman was summoned by the President to evaluate the potential of a team consisting of Matt, mathematician, and his wealthy grandfather, the General, to solve an important problem regarding the pandemic that has disrupted the world order. The woman's positive opinion leads the President to proceed with the team to solve the problem.

Matt and the General are avid golfers. They are called to the White House to solve a problem that is important to the President of the United States, and the remainder of the free world. The team plans to go to the White House to further investigate the situation.

The team is given an additional recommendation by the Chairman of the Joint Chiefs of Staff. It proceeds in the General's personal jet to Langley Field and then to the President's private office.

The President outlines his problem that encompasses researching data related to the pandemic for three tasks: the state of the union message to the people, the upcoming election, and the government report on the pandemic. Matt and the General accept the challenge and form a team to attack the problem.

Matt and the General meet with the President concerning a planned project organization concerning the pandemic. A former associate of Matt and the General known as Amelia Robinson, attended the meeting. Her behavior is unusual for a government employee. Matt mentions the incident to Ashley, who noticed that she is a Russian shopper characteristic of a Russian mole.

Matt and the General have mixed emotions on the project, so the President suggests a meeting in Camp David highlighted by the construction, in four days, of a small golf course. Matt and the General are persuaded to continue with the project and travel to Camp David for the meeting.

The team prepares for the trip to Camp David, and Anna prepares a introductory paper on pandemics for the President. Matt and Ashley attempt to analyze the President's motives and they come up with a possible solution to the pandemic problem. The team travels to Camp David and gets settled into their roles. The Amelia Russian deal is resolved and President considers running her as a mole in Russia, as this might be the origin of the virus.

Travel to Washington is set up, and the President reveals the plan to run Amelia as a mole. The General meets with Sir Charles Bunday, known as Buzz, to discuss the purpose of the project and covers the progress so far. Matt gives the guidelines and a good summary of progress made so far. Amelia and her role in Russia are discussed.

Matt and Ashley relate the total solution to the General, and they advise the President of that solution. It seems as though a Russian scientist is the cause the problem and dies before his anecdote can be developed. This is covered later.

Amelia gets an academic slot in Ohio in a university think tank."

"I have something to say before I leave the stage, so to speak," said Daniel. "I did not enjoy this project at all. The pandemic and how it is being solved is just too complicated and too frustrating; there are a lot of good people just spinning their wheels. Trying very hard and essentially getting nowhere. In reality, who cares where it came from. Let's just solve the vaccine situation get on with our lives. Thank you."

"Thanks Daniel," said I guy in the middle of the room. "It's a tough subject and you did a remarkable job. We would like to thank you for giving your time and effort. Especially while you were flying down to Australia."

The members of the Romeo Club gave Daniel Robertson a hearty round of applause."

Steve Smith had a big problem. He had given Matt the last three sessions. Two were conspiracy theories on the origin of pandemic and the third is an update of what the government is doing on the emerging problem of artificial intelligence. Perhaps, there are other possible presentations that are not about the pandemic. He was tired of the pandemic and if he heard the word COVID one more time, he would do something but he was unsure of what it was.

END OF CHAPTER FOURTEEN

Chapter 15

From Russia with Love

Matt had been thinking about the virus and its by-products that resulted in a lot of terrible misfortune to those that were infected by the virus and their associated families and friends. We are here at the Romeo Club so as to leave with a good feeling from time well spent. There is definitely too much doom and gloom. So let's get over it and on to something else. So, I have a couple of short stories that should be interesting to all of my retired friends. So when he was introduced by Steve Smith, he started right in.

"Good morning, my name is Matt Miller and I am here to finish your fine breakfast with a curious story. Actually, I have two stories, and if I have the time, I will cover both. Otherwise, the second will have to wait. So here goes, and I am speaking in the first person, whatever that means. I only teach math.

The President of the United States asked Matt, Ashley, and the General to help him with a problem concerned with the virus that was just starting to pose less of a threat. He needed information for his state of the union speech, a government report, and his personal archive. The trio covered the epidemic quite well and encountered a Russian mole – that is a person who lives in Russia and feeds information back to the states. Apparently, she obtained knowledge of a well-known scientist that wanted to earn a noble prize. He came up with an ingenious plan. If a person invented a cure for the virus, he or she would for sure get that prize. The scientist was very well regarded in Russia and the entire world for knowledge and research on various problems in the area of biology related to infectious diseases. He determined that he could create in his lab a serum to give a person the COVID disease. He knew, based on his research, how to create an antidote to cure the disease.

Here was his plan. His country like all the rest, has training programs that prepare potential spies with needed information about a country, its customs and speech habits, and local ways of saying things. Each of the potential spies was sent to the country as a student, for practice in their spying capability. He had his own research facility .and could enable this plan. It was his plan and only his plan. He would infect a student through his or her favorite drink, like coca cola. He would send them to them to the various countries and infect the people. Of course, the virus would spread rapidly. They would go all over the free and non-free world. He could only get the Nobel Prize if people all over the world were infected.

His students would go into the world and infected many people. Through propagation of the disease, it would spread quickly. The students would come back to Russia and he would give them the antidote. However, in the process, he infected himself and died before he could finalize the antidote. None of the leadership of Russia and the Premier knew about this insidious plan. And that is the origin of the virus.

Matt figured out the insidious plan and Matt, Ashley, the General informed the President of the scheme. Here is the result.

A white House jet took the General, Matt, and Ashley to Andrews Air force Base and Marine One, escorted by three other helicopters, took them to the White House lawn, The President met them at the exit from the Marine One helicopter, and they were escorted by the Secret Service to the President's private office.

The General described the pandemic situation for the President, who listened intently for the duration of the presentation, which was supplemented by remarks from Matt and Ashley.

The President's only remark was, "The situation should never be put into writing. It looks like your job is finished. I wanted you to tell me what I should talk about in my various addresses, and you just told me exactly what not to talk about. Thank you."

"And that," said Matt. "Is the end of the presentation. Of course, it is all made up to inform and amuse you. I'll be right back. I drank too much coffee. I have to go to the gent."

Ashley asked the General, "What is gent."

The General looked her with a smile, "Instead of using a bathroom or rest room or loo or something like that, gentlemen use the word **gent** for gentleman's room. Got it?"

Ashley just smiled, little boys make up their own words.

END OF CHAPTER FIFTEEN

CHAPTER 16

From Outer Space with Love

Matt was back in a jiffy. He was definitely enjoying himself. Again, the back of the restaurant was lined with staff and visitors. Ashley looked around and smiled. She was more than proud of her husband. Most of the audience sat up in their chairs. In Matt's absence, the restaurant served free coffee. This was good advertising, and interesting as well. The good thing about Matt's presentations was that he wasn't giving a lecture, but it was a simple conversation.

"This presentation will definitely be of interest to most, if not all, of you. It involves technology, space science, and the virus that has hopefully passed us by," remarked Matt. "It is not complicated but boy is it interesting. Fasten your seat belts."

"It all started for me anyway when the CIA released its library of information on UFOs. It perked my interest in what was actually going on in that area of technology. People have been recording experiences for years now, and as yet we have no indication of what is going on. Farmers see them, pilots see them, and seemingly every one else has seen one. They always have their lights on. Even the General has seen one when he was a P-51 pilot during World War II. Now here is a question. Let's say I purchase a recreational drone and attach a flashlight to it. Do I have a UFO drone? Most of you would say absolutely NO. Then what is a UFO? I will look into that first, and then carry on.

At first I thought that the lights were part of the propulsion system that keeps the UFO up. There were 2780 CIA reports on the subject so it was hard to go through all of that stuff, and also, some of the reports had some sentences blacked out for security reasons. There was a series of events that opened the door on this subject. The university that I teach at wanted to open a research lab for Astrophysics in New Jersey. The scientists were American but the director was a person named Michael Davis, usually know as Prince Michael of the English monarchy, who has a PhD from Oxford and is quite an intelligent fellow. He was not treated nicely in addition to a temperament that did not blend well with American workers. He was not used to handling equipment and did not work long hours like most Americans. On one occasion he used the wrong equipment on the right thing or vice versa. He got interesting information, which I will cover later, and the Americans must have said the wrong thing to him. His personal life did not exist. So one day he just left and went back to England without telling anyone. The English thought he was bonkers. The paparazzi and the media got hold of the story and then he was really bonkers. He handled the vaccine quite well in England. There was something going on upstairs with him – that is, his brain – and we decided to look into it. We thought that we would not be able to get anything out of him but perhaps his mum, the retired queen, could. That was arranged and some very useful information came out of it.

As part of the equipment mix-up, some interesting information was revealed. Prince Michael explained it as follows:

> "It started out as a simple equipment error. I was going to use an astrophysics electron camera and focused it at a close distance rather than a far distance. It was a common error, as I was not accustomed to using the equipment. I viewed a large squadron of space vehicles headed for Earth. There was a very high number of them, and they appeared to be in complete synchronicity, probably driven by one computer or by individual computers operating in exactly the same way. The formation was without any deviation. Some of them were lighted as UFOs normally are. I focused the electron camera outward and observed that the squadron was emanating from within another galaxy.
>
> It appeared to be from the Pinwheel Galaxy that has a planet Zenex with identical characteristics to Earth. The lighted UFOs appeared to be leaders, and the others could be controlled by artificial entities."

Here is how my thinking progressed. After the 1950s incident when a UFO crashed and the Army took it to area 51, and we never heard anything about it. After that, Boeing, then called the Boeing Airplane Company, had a project to develop a Closed Ecological System (CES) sponsored by the Defense Department. It was a cold war method for survival. In a CES, humans could live for an extended period in an enclosure containing water, plants, and a crop of fish. The humans could eat the fish. The planets could absorb the carbon monoxide, and so forth. The system was actually built and tested there.

People could survive for an extended period of time. No more information exists on CES to my knowledge.

The UFOs with lights could be surveying the planet Earth and return to the Pinwheel Galaxy in a CES. It's pretty far back, about 21 million light years. A light year is the distance that light can travel in a year. But, time slows down at very high speeds so it is possible.

Then Zenex space ships, piloted by artificial intelligence and using nuclear power could be distributing phenomena, such as the COVID virus, to the entire world. When we are all killed, the inhabitants of their planet in the Pinwheel Galaxy, which is going extinct, could be transferred to Earth through a large number of CESs in space ships powered by nuclear engines and controlled by artificial intelligence.

There could be two types of UFOs: a lighted one that would transport human occupants, and a dark one that transports viruses and is driven by computers, and destroys itself over the ocean.

The President responded by saying that the U.S. Team has planned a new military force named the SPACE FORCE that will be announced to the public in two days. It should protect the planet Earth and the United States against spatial invasion of any kind."

That, said Matt, is the end of my story. Believe it or not. Thanks for your kind attention.

The Romeo audience and the folks at the back of the restaurant sat there expressionless for a few seconds, and then gave an honest applause.

END OF CHAPTER SIXTEEN

Chapter 17

The Terrorist Event

Steve Smith introduced Daniel Robertson, their Australia traveler, and the retired old men in the room said in union, "Hi Daniel. Glad you're back." Those Romeo guys sure are cheerful this morning, thought Steve Smith the Romeo leader, so to speak.

"I'm glad to be back," said Daniel. "And today was the best breakfast I've had in a while.

I have several little stories and we will see if we can fit them in. If not, Steve said we could add another breakfast. Without further ado, I'll get started."

The group, that is Matt, Ashley, the General, and Anna, were in Coligny Plaza on Hilton Head Island. The ladies were looking in the shops for something, but it wasn't clear what that was. Matt and the General were just wandering, when a group of young guys cut in front of them. Matt and the General had to stop to let them go by. Remember, I'm talking in the first person. It feels strange.

Those Hispanics think they own the place, remarked the General.

They're not Hispanic, said Matt. They are Iranians. You can tell by the way their faces are shaped, their beards, their physical structure, their hair, and who knows what else. They hang around together and talk incessantly. One of our students at the university wrote a paper on them. They get into the country illegally and come in through places with open beaches and an older population that doesn't pay attention to the population. That could be Hilton Head Island.

"What do you think they are doing here?" asked the General.

Who knows, said Matt. They don't work but seem to have money. Their wives hang out in coffee places after their kids leave for school, just like Americans. The government tries to keep track of them but there are too many, and it doesn't know exactly how they get in, if it is exactly true that is how they get in. This is just a supposition.

The government does a good job of it, and this is just one of the cases they have uncovered. It was an attempt to bomb the White House. The plot was uncovered and resolved and practically no one knew about it. Here is a summary.

The action is centered on Hilton Head Island in beautiful South Carolina. Some terrorists with their families have gained entry to the United States through illegal means and reside in in Hilton Head. The Iranian director of the project lives in a separate house, because he requires 5G communication lines that are not available elsewhere. The other workers families, and kids, live in separate luxury apartments, and meet regularly in a local coffee house. The essence of this terrorist attack is to crash a large airplane loaded with jet fuel into the White House.

The White House is closely protected against air attacks, so the terrorists developed and ingenious plan. The terrorists needed three airplanes to execute their plan, along with an unused area of Pease Air Force base in New Hampshire. Three of the Iranians buy the three planes needed for their operation based in New Hampshire from a plane graveyard in New Mexico. The planes are flown surreptitiously during the night to Pease air base where they are modified to be pilotless aircraft using artificial intelligence methods. The plan is to crash one plane into the Air Traffic Control Center in Boston to prevent Boston from passing information on a suspicious aircraft into the Air Traffic Control Center in Washington.

The Washington Air Traffic Control Center is destroyed as a result of the second pilotless aircraft. The operation leaves Washington unprotected against an incoming terrorist plane loaded with fuel that is highly flammable. It too is pilotless and is supposed to crash in to the White House.

Matt figures out the plan and has the three pilotless planes destroyed by American tactical fighter planes, and the White House is saved. It is a major accomplishment and Matt is duly recognized as a hero and is appropriately rewarded by the President of the United States.

The terrorist leader agrees to do spy work for the Americans, after he is apprehended by the police. The Iranian workers and their families escape to Iran, and the episode ends with the Air Traffic control Centers and the White House intact.

And that is the end of the story.

*****

Daniel Robertson excuses himself and says he has to hit the head. One of the waitresses says to Ashley, "What is the head?' Ashley replies, "It is what little boys call the bathroom."

END OF CHAPTER SEVENTEEN

CHAPTER 18

An Information Leak

Daniel Robertson picked up where he left off. In this story he encounters an information leak that is very important to the country. A new defensive capability is developed and tested and information on that system has been leaked to a magazine. How could this happen? We will find out.

A new high-speed pilotless fighter plane is being flown. It is attached to a B-52 and lifted to about 600 feet and released. It is escorted by a fast fighter plane to 2½ times the speed of sound. It is designed to engage the enemy and then return to the take off point. Since the fighter is pilotless, American lives are not in jeopardy. It is referred to as the F/A plane and is planned to be the American fighter plane of the future.

The commanding officers were more than pleased and sent appropriate messages to the President and the Pentagon. Two days later, the following description was described by an aircraft magazine:

The American Air Force has successfully flown the new pilotless F/A plane at Mach 2.5 and it successfully returned to the air base. The U.S. Military Command was pleased.

There was no further announcement. Some readers thought the news item was strategic posturing and others regarded it to be a serious information leak. Regardless of the reason, the news release was considered to be a serious security problem by military officials.

The President was more than furious and ordered his Chief of Staff to contact General Mark Clark. His request was short and simple, "We have a major leak in the advanced military information system, and we need the immediate service of your advanced security team, known as Matt and the General. Get them here as soon as possible.

At first, they thought the leak came from Area 51, that worked on advanced projects, but Matt was convinced the problem came from Seattle. Also, he thought it was from someone that did not work with the aircraft system on a daily basis. A person who worked on the project would know it was important. Someone outside of the project was probably the cause of the leak. A security worker who had previously worked for the aircraft company was interviewed. He was familiar with the Highway 99 Lehman Field area, He remembered working at Lehman Field and watched military planes and high speed chase planes operate in the area. Down the road from the plant was a medium-sized restaurant frequented by employees. That was all of the information that Matt needed.

"That's it," said Matt. "Position Adam Benfield, our new intelligence person, at the restaurant and let him talk to the customers on an informal basis. Adam Benfield looks foreign and would be interested in the American way of life. People like to talk, especially after a good dinner."

The identification took only a week, when Adam started talking to a young fellow who customarily ate there.

"Hi, I'm Adam," said Adam.

"I'm Robert," said the young fellow. "Robert Bostonovic."

"What do you do?" asked Adam.

"I fly a high-speed chase plane here at Lehman," said Robert. "I was an F-15 pilot in the Air Force in the Viet Nam war."

"What do you do here?" asked Adam.

"I fly chase aircraft and usually photograph other planes during flight," answered Robert, "such as the F/A pilotless airplane that flew last week – maybe the week before."

"That's interesting," said Adam. "I would like to find out about things like that. "I'm a military buff. My father was in the service. I flew bombers myself, but that was years ago."

"There is a complete description of that F/A plane in *Aircraft and Space Technology*," said Robert. "I helped write it. There was reporter from the Times in here and was also interested in things like that."

Adam signaled the controller, seated nearby, and Robert was arrested as a probable suspect with no resistance. All he said was, "I didn't want to do anything bad. I'm sorry."

When the word got back to Matt and the General, Matt said, "The easiest solution is often the best one."

"You can say that again," said the General.

END OF CHAPTER EIGHTEEN

CHAPTER 19

Ransomware

Daniel Robertson was ready to go again, after a couple of bytes of his blueberry pancake. The Romeo audience liked him, because of his back home attitude. He was totally relaxed in front of the crowd. For *Ransomware* he needed notes.

"This is a summary of my reading on ransomware; one of the persons that worked for me had a problem of this type so I looked it up. I'll start with some introductory material as if you have never heard of it," said Robertson. A man is the back of the tables said, "I've never heard of it so the more the better."

"It's when a dishonest person gets into your computer and takes over the software and locks the data files using cryptography and you have to pay to have them unlocked – hence the name *ransomware*. Sometimes, the files are important, like in a hospital, but not all of the time. Students that had their files locked asked what to do and were told to just reload the system software. But, when it involves infrastructure computers, like with oil companies, electric suppliers, and hospitals, the situation gets serious and the company just pays the requested money. It has already been as high as a million dollars. Sometimes the criminals lock the entire computer. It seems there is a conceptual model behind the criminal use of ransomware and it is something like the following. A computer operator get bored in the middle of the night just sitting there and handling computer operations. He searches on the Internet until he gets an interesting link and then he clicks on it. The malware, as it is called, is loaded and takes over the computer.

Here is how it works. Some event happens and the malware is loaded onto the computer to be invaded. It is well written software usually called smart software. It starts looking around until it finds something interesting. It uses its cryptographic software to lock the data file or database. It threatens that it will destroy the data and requests money to unlock it. Customers could be large or small, but large customers are a good target.

This is a terrible problem because users like a hospital are involved the people's lives are at stake. The users usually have to pay using bitcoin and the U.S. government is on their tail. Some of the bad guys are in Russia because the government has no law against doing it. However, the Russian government is not involved with it and is also known to be the victim.

Major software companies are addressing the problem.

And that is it. Thank you very much.

Steve Smith stood up and thanked Daniel for his efforts. The people in the room gave him a big applause for his hard work. Steve thanks the men for their attendance and wished them a great summer.

END OF CHAPTER NINETEEN

CHAPTER 20

And That's the End of the Story

Steve Smith, the director of Romeo, stood up after a delicious breakfast and welcomed the gang to the last meeting of Retired Old Men Eating Out before the summer break. "Welcome to our last breakfast of the year. We've had a great year and the presentations have been more than excellent. Let's give a hand to all of the speakers. I've taken the liberty to give the last presentation, because I think it is a good heart-warming story. It is a true story that gives you a look at human nature. I have checked with Matt, the General, and their confidant Ashley Miller; they assured me that the story would be appropriate and interesting to the ROMEO group. So, let's get started."

It happened to a close friend of mine; actually a college roommate. His name is Walter Baldwin. We studied our math together, and through his wit and temperament, we both did well. He has a good and beautiful wife, an outstanding son, and an also beautiful daughter, named Kimberly Baldwin. This is really her story.

Kimberly met Sam Peterson in a freshman psychology course. He asked her if she would like a cup of coffee with him at the local Starbucks, and she said yes. He was a nice boy, not particularly handsome by American standards, but active and friendly. He was on the soccer team and could run like the wind. Most of all, he was very attentive to Kimberly; he was a good catch. Kimberly was a nursing student and Sam liked that; he frequently asked her about her nursing studies. Kimberly desired a career in emergency nursing, and the money was good. It was a tough job and the hours would be long. Sam didn't seem to mind.

Kimberly and Sam dated together for four years and they graduated at the same time. Kimberly chose a hospital in St. Louis and by chance Sam got an engineering job in the same city. Things went well but an engagement never came.

One Christmas, Sam's mother visited Kimberly and told her that Sam would be going to visit his brother in Iran to work on an engineering problem that was in trouble. At first, Kimberly was totally shocked. She loved Sam and she thought he loved her. What was happening? Why hadn't Sam told her personally. Finally, Sam's mother told Kimberly that they were Iranian and had adopted the common English name of Peterson. Kimberly was devastated but soon got over it. Sam was just afraid to tell Kimberly that he was Iranian; he loved her so much and was afraid that she would reject him. Kimberly told Sam's mother that she still loved Sam and that everything would be okay when Sam returned to the U.S.

Then, out of the blue, Sam's mother called Kimberly and said that Sam was deathly ill and needed her attention. Kimberly really loved Sam; he was so kind and gentle and always good with financial affairs. She had to go, much to her father's concern. He said no, and she said yes, and she won.

Kimberly flew first class to Iran with Lufthansa and was met at the airport in Tehran. The driver spoke no English and Kimberly spoke no Farsi. They arrived at the central hospital and Sam met Kimberly at the entrance. Kimberly was surprised that he wasn't sick. He gave her a give American hug and said, "I'm glad you are here. Now we are together for life."

Kimberly was shocked. For life? No. Her father was right. At her first opportunity, he sent a message to her father explaining the situation. She was totally surprised. Her father was as cool as a cucumber. All he said in a message was, "I'll take care of it."

Walter Baldwin called his former commanding officer by the name of Gen. Les Miller. Baldwin was also a general officer in the military. "Les, I have a problem. Can you help?"

General officers are a brand of their own. They take care of each other. General Baldwin explained the situation to General Miller. All the General said was, "We'll take care of it. We have experience dealing with those rascals. It'll take a few days. She'll be okay."

The general called Matt and explained the situation with Matt. He asked Matt to take care of the drone and he would ask Adam Benfield to give assistance, since he was Iranian and knew what to do.

"Adam, I have a job for you. You are still registered as a spy on Iran. Is that right?"

"I am," said Adam. "They send me a check every month. They do not expect anything from me. I told them I have HIV and they are deathly afraid of me. I still have all connections in Tehran waiting for me to come home."

"I know the drill General. How many people will be involved from your end?"

"I don't know yet." answered the General. "I'll check with Matt and Ashley. She will probably need a female escort."

The General got on his old military phone and contacted his old student friend Robert Peterson, the Iranian Vice President for whom he and Matt arranged the shipment of COVID vaccine that saved the country if Iran. Robert Peterson asked the General who the bad guy in Iran and the General said it was Sam Peterson."

Robert Peterson, the General's old school buddy answered, "He is my son. Sorry Les. You saved our country, and I'll take care of it on this end. We'll do an extraction on a holiday weekend."

Matt found that the special passenger drones were sitting idle in the drone base in Israel. He arranged for a passenger drone pilot that would be on call when the plans were worked.

Without any incident whatsoever, Matt, Ashley, and the General were flown to the Israel drone base.

So, as it worked out, Matt, the General, and Ashley, were dressed in military uniforms. The General was a Four-Star General, Matt was a Colonel, and Ashley was a Major. They flew to the abandoned Iranian Sukhoi airfield in a drone, and were picked up by Adam Benfield in his Mercedes S500 and transported to a luxury hotel in Tehran. Benfield had flow to Iran by Lufthansa earlier. They were met at the hotel by Kimberly Baldwin and the Iranian vice present Robert Peterson. It was a happy meeting even though the people did not know each other. After a nice Iranian dinner, they have the world's best food – so they say, we steal it from everybody, the team slept in appropriate accommodations and were transported back to Sukhoi in a new Mercedes SUV. The drone to ride to Israel was without incident and they all, including Kimberly and Adam Benfield, were flown back to the states in the General's S550.

All the General said was, "We did our job, case closed."

All the Steve Smith said was, "Thank you everybody."

The retired old men gathered around Matt, Ashley, and the General with congratulations. It was the most unusual story they had ever heard in their short Romeo lives.

END OF CHAPTER TWENTY

CHAPTER 21

Artificial Intelligence

Steve Smith called the General and said that he hadn't had a chance to round up a speaker for the next meeting. He wondered if John Gelder might be willing to give a talk on Artificial Intelligence. The subject had been growing in popularity. The General said that he could not think of a reason that it was inappropriate. So, Steve called John Gelder, who mentioned he was quite busy at the time with the rapid growth of artificial intelligence, but he could give the same talk as before. Steve said okay and John was on the docket. John arrived early with a large load of copies, and Steve Smith announced him with great pleasure. The fellows in the audience were more than pleased.

"This time I bought more than enough copies of my presentation for all of you fine gentlemen," said John Gelder. "If you want a copy to read while I talk, there are copies at various places in the room. It is the same talk as before. I'm as busy with artificial intelligence as I've ever been, and I apologize for that."

As before, the title of my presentation in artificial intelligence.

Overview

The question, Can a machine think?" is one that has been debated for some time now and the question is no likely to be answered in this book. However, the subject is fruitful when considering what a computer can do."

There are various opinions on the subject. Some say that thinking is an activity that is peculiar to human beings. Accordingly, machines cannot think. Although thought as something unique to humans may have been in the minds of early philosophers when they first considered the subject of thinking and intelligence, this does not really define the activity. Others maintain that a machine is thinking when it is performing activities that normally require thought when performed by human beings. Thus, adding 2+3 must be a form of thinking. To continue, some psychologists have defined have defined intelligence in the following simple way: intelligence is what an intelligence test measures. In light of the preceding section on information systems, all that needs to be done is to feed enough information into an information system and to develop an appropriate query language, and the result is an intelligent machine. This line of reasoning also skirts a clear definition. Perhaps, it is a waste of time to worry about precise definitions, but the fact remains that computers are doing some amazing things - such as playing chess, guiding robots, controlling space vehicles, recognizing patterns, proving theorems, and answering questions - and that these applications require much more than the conventional computer program. Richard Hamming, developer of the prestigious Hamming code for error detection and correction in computers, gives a definition of intelligent behavior that may be useful here:

The ability to act in subtle ways when presented with a class of situations that have not been exhaustively analyzed in advance, but which require rather different combinations of responses if the result in many specific cases is to be acceptable.

Artificial Intelligence is an important subject because it may indicate the direction in which society is moving. Currently, machines are used for two reasons: (1) The job cannot be done by a human being, and (2) The job can be performed more economically by a machine. To this list, another reason must be added: some jobs are simply too dull to be done by humans, and it is desirable from a social point of view to have such jobs done by machine. This requires a greater number of "intelligent" machines, since people seem to be finding more and more work they consider to be dull and routine. Here are two items of interest before we get started with the talk:

Artificial general intelligence (AGI) is the intelligence of a machine that could successfully perform any intellectual task that a human being can. It is a primary goal of some AI research and is a common topic in science fiction and future studies. (Author unknown.)

The singularity is the hypothesis that the invention of artificial super intelligence (ASI) *will abruptly trigger runaway technical growth, resulting in unfathomable change to human civilization.* (Author unknown,)

It is possible to approach Artificial Intelligence from two points of view. Both approaches make use of programs and programming techniques. The first approach is to investigate the general principles of intelligence. The second is to study human thought, in particular.

Those persons engaged in the investigation of the principles of intelligence are normally charged with the development of systems that appear to be intelligent. This activity is commonly regarded as "artificial intelligence," which incorporates both engineering and computer science components.

Those same persons engaged in the study of human thought attempt to emulate human mental processes to a lesser or greater degree. This activity can be regarded as a form of "computer simulation," such that the elements of a relevant psychological theory are represented in a computer program. The objective of this approach is to generate psychological theories of human thought. The discipline is generally known as "Cognitive Science."

In reality, the differences between artificial intelligence and cognitive science tend to vary between "not so much" and "quite a lot" - depending upon the complexity of the underlying task. Most applications, as a matter of fact, contain elements from both approaches.

The Scope of AI

It is possible to zoom in on the scope of AI by focusing on the processes involved. At one extreme, the concentration is on the practicalities of doing AI programming, with an emphasis on symbolic programming languages and AI machines. In this context, AI can be regarded as a new way of doing programming. It necessarily follows that hardware/software systems with AI components have the potential for enhanced end-user effectiveness,

At the other extreme, AI could be regarded as the study of intelligent computation. This is a more grandiose and encompassing focus with the objective of building a systematic and encompassing focus with the objective of building a systematic theory of intellectual processes - regardless if they model human thought or not.

It would appear, therefore, that AI is more concerned with intelligence in general and less involved with human thought in particular. Thus, it may be contended that humans and computers are simply two options in the genus of information processing systems.

The Modern Era of Artificial Intelligence

The modern era of artificial intelligence effectively began with the summer conference at Dartmouth College in Hanover, New Hampshire in 1956. The key participants were Shannon from Bell Labs, Minsky from Harvard (later M.I.T.), McCarthy from Dartmouth (later M.I.T. and Stanford), and Simon from Carnegie Tech (renamed Carnegie Mellon). The key results from the conference were twofold:

- It legitimized the notion of AI and brought together a raft of piecemeal research activities.
- The name "Artificial Intelligence" was coined and the name more thy anything had a profound influence of the future direction of artificial intelligence.

The stars of the conference were Simon, and his associate Allen Newell, who demonstrated the Logic Theorist - the first well-known reasoning program. They preferred the name, "Complex Information Processing," for the new fledging science of the artificial. In the end, Shannon and McCarthy won out with the zippy and provocative name, "artificial intelligence." In all probability, the resulting controversy surrounding the name artificial intelligence served to sustain a certain critical mass of academic interest in the subject - even during periods of sporadic activity and questionable results.

One of the disadvantages of the pioneering AI conference was the simple fact that an elite group of scientists was created that would effectively decide "what AI is and what AI isn't," and how to best achieve it. The end result was that AI became closely aligned with psychology and not with neurophysiology and to a lesser degree with electrical engineering. AI became a software science with the main objective of producing intelligent artifacts. In short, it became a closed group, and this effectively constrained the field for a large degree.

In recent years, the direction of AI research has been altered somewhat by an apparent relationship with brain research and cognitive technology, which is known as the design of joint human-machine cognitive systems. Two obvious fallouts of the new direction are the well-known "Connection Machine," and the computer vision projects at the National

Bureau of Standards in their United States. That information is somewhat out of date, but the history gives some insight into what AI is today and where it will be heading.

Early Work on the Concept of Artificial Intelligence

The history of AI essentially goes back to the philosophy of Plato, who wrote that. "All knowledge must be state able in explicit definitions which anyone could apply," thereby eliminating appeals to judgment and intuition. Plato's student Aristotle continued in this noble tradition in the development of the categorical syllogism, which plays an important part in modern logic.

The mathematician Leibnitz attempted to quantify all knowledge and reasoning through an exact algebraic system by which all objects are assigned a unique characteristic number. Using these characteristic numbers, therefore, rules for the combination of problems would be establishes and controversies could be resolved by calculation.

The underlying philosophical idea was conceptually simple: Reduce the whole of human knowledge into a single formal system. The notion of formal representation has become the basis of AI and cognitive science theories since it involves the reduction of the totality of human experience to a set of basic elements that can be glued together in various ways.

To sum up, the philosophical phenomenologists argue that it impossible to subject pure phenomena - i.e., mental acts which give meaning to the world - to formal analysis. Of course, AI people do not agree. They contend that "there is no ghost in the machine," and this is meant to imply that intelligence is a set of well-defined physical processes.

The discussion is reminiscent of the mind/brain controversy and it appears that the AI perspective is that "the mind is what the brain does." Of course, the phenomenologists would reply that the definition of mind exists beyond the physical neurons; it also incorporates the intangible concepts of what the neurons do.

Accordingly, *strong AI* is defined in the literature as the case wherein an appropriately programmed computer actually is a "mind." *Weak AI*, on the other hand is the emulation of human intelligence, as we know it.

Intelligence and Intelligent Systems

There seems to be some value in the ongoing debate over the intelligence of AI artifacts. The term "artificial" in artificial intelligence helps us out. One could therefore contend that intelligence is natural if it is biological and artificial otherwise. This conclusion skirts the controversy and frees intellectual energy for more purposeful activity.

The abstract notion of intelligence, therefore, is conceptualized, and natural and artificial intelligence serve as specific instances. The subjects of understanding and learning could be treated in a similar manner. The productive tasks of identifying the salient aspects of intelligence, understanding, and learning emerge as the combined goal of AI and cognitive science. For example, the concepts of representation and reasoning, to name only two of many, have been studied productively from both artificial and biological viewpoints. Software products that are currently available can be evaluated in the basis of how well they can support the basic AI technologies, The key question then becomes: How well do natural and artificial systems, as discussed above, match up to the abstract notion of intelligence.

Cognitive Technology

Cognitive technology is the set of concepts and techniques for developing joint human-machine cognitive systems. People are obviously interested in cognitive systems because they are goal directed and employ self-knowledge of the environment to monitor, plan, and modify their actions in the pursuit of their goals. In a logical sense, joint human-machine systems can also be classed as being cognitive because of the availability of computational techniques for automating decisions and exercising operational control over physical processes and organizational activities.

Recent advances in heuristic techniques coupled with methods of knowledge representation and automated reasoning have made it possible to couple human cognitive systems with artificial cognitive systems. Accordingly, joint systems in this case would necessarily have the following attributes:

- Be problem driven, rather than technology driven.
- Effective models of underlying processes are needed.
- Control of decision-making processes must be shared between human and artificial components.

Clearly, cognitive technology represents a possible (if not probable) paradigm shift whereby the human self-view can and wake in the not-too-distant future.

Virtual Systems and Imagination

Methods for reasoning in expert and cognitive systems are well defined. Rules and representation effectively solve the problem. There appears to be a set of problems, however, that seem to evade such a simple solution as rules and representation.

A sophisticated model of a cognitive system must incorporate the capability of reasoning about itself or another cognitive system and about the computational facilities that provide the cognition. When a person, for example, is asked to reason about the feelings of the probable response of another person, set of rules is normally invoked to provide the desired response. If no rule set exists, then a virtual process is engaged that proceeds somewhat as follows:

- The object process is imagined, i.e. you effectively put yourself in the other person's shoes, so to speak.
- The neural inputs are "faked" and the brain responds in somewhat the same manner as it would in real life.
- The result is observed exactly as though it had taken place.

Thus, a sort of simulation of a self-model is employed. This type of analysis might be invoked if someone were asked, for example, how they would feel if they had just received the news they had contracted an incurable disease.

The process, described above, is essentially what an operating system does while controlling the execution of a "guest" operating system. Inputs and outputs are interpreted, but machine code is actually executed.

It necessarily follows that executable models, as suggested here, are as much a form of knowledge as are rules and facts.

But, Is It intelligent?

Bandying the issue even further, a sharp borderline between intelligent and non-intelligent behavior, in the abstract sense, probably does not exist. Nevertheless, some essential qualities might be the following:

- To respond to situations very flexibly.
- To take advantage of fortuitous circumstances.
- To make sense out of ambiguous or contradictory messages.
- To recognize the relative importance of different elements of a situation.
- To find similarities between situations despite differences which may separate them.
- To draw distinctions between situations despite similarities which may link them.
- To synthesize new concepts by taking old concepts and putting them together in new ways.
- To come up with ideas that are novel.

Viewed in this manner, intelligence is a form of computation. Effective intelligence then is a process (perhaps a computer program) and an appropriate machine in which to execute the process.

Systems Concepts and AI

An interesting viewpoint the concerns the evolution of data processing has emerged from the AI business. The task of designing a rule base and an associate fact base is somewhat analogous to designing an information system. Moreover, both kinds of systems appear to evolve in a similar manner. For this analysis, it should be assumed that statements and computational processes (i.e., modules) are the same (or synonymous).

A sensory stimulation is associated with a statement. (Incidentally, this concept is known as *associations,* wherein a sensation is associated with an idea, and that idea leads to another idea, and so forth. This theory originated with Aristotle and was pursued by Hobbs, Locke, and Mill.). The associations reverberate through the system of statements, whereby a result is finally achieved. The output can viewed as a prediction. Moreover, the system operates according to some form internal laws - such as the laws of mathematics.

When a prediction fails, continuing with the statement analogy, we question the validity of the set of statements. Revisions are normally in order. Since a direct correlation is usually possible between the stimuli and peripheral statements, these statements are preserved from revision.

Other statements must bear the brunt of change. The *other* statements, however, can be regarded as the "frozen middle," since they result from internal laws. The end result that a priority judgment. Is necessary: change the peripheral statements of change the frozen middle. The priorities of course are in conflict and the preference commonly goes to the revision that disturbs the system the least.

Effectively, incremental changes are made to the system until a total revision is necessary - i.e., a rewrite of the internal including the Laws, the frozen middle, and the peripheral statements. As a total concept, major revisions serve to simplify a system. It necessarily follows that some attention should be given to systems evolution as a predictive technique.

Thank you for the time. As you noted, I am passionate about the subject.

The audience of retired men absolutely enjoy the presentation. One guy whistled, everyone clapped. One gentleman said, "I wish I were young again, I would study AI." Another said, "I wish I had a recording of your talk."

END OF CHAPTER TWENTY-ONE

Chapter 22

Thinking About Artificial Intelligence

The subject of Artificial Intelligence is in the news almost every day. Ordinarily people, business, schools, and even religious organizations have taken up the subject. This is a short chapter giving items a lot a people would/should know about the subject. A brief survey of Artificial Intelligence was given in Chapter 21. Artificial Intelligence Ontology is introduced in this chapter and covered in more detail in chapter 23.

AI Commitment

The subject covers safety assessments, equity and civil right guidance and research on AI's impact on the operational and labor markets. The implication is this is what the political leader or business leader should do without being excessively demanding. There are 25 things. Remember, I just thought this stuff up and I am just a math professor. The emphasize is on the abuses of AI.

Safety Standards and Security Requirements for AI Software:

- Tests
- Guidelines for duplication
- AI tools to identify rules in underlying software.

Privacy

- What techniques are used in software and operations.

Civil Rights

- Guidance to landlords and contractors
- AI methods and discrimination
- The justice system, of sentence systems and risk methods

Consumer Protection

- Health and human services
- Potential harmful AI related health-care practices

Workers and the Labor Market

- Effect on the labor market from AI
- Support workers and job affected

AI Business

- Potential labor market of AI
- Government related protection

AI Research Innovation

- Grants for AI research
- Selection control
- Innovative AI workers

Federal agencies cooperation

These are guideline to restrict unnecessary competition and help to protect customers from venders that can't support a diverse client base.

What we need is the cooperation of AI companies with voluntary commitment tom control developments and needless cooperation, and we need regulation for this. The management of risk and support for federal needs are paramount. Large Ai companies should cooperate and not compete on test results. Training data should be shared between competitors to develop a dependable workforce. Lastly, the competitive vendors should accelerate developments so as to limit the entry of potential vendors that cannot support a customer base.

AI Planning

The AI has to match the organizational structure in order to determine what has to be done.

AI has to do at least what people do now.

How can AI go into an organization and match intelligent objects with manual objects. How is AI able to see what is going on. Remember that AI should be intelligent enough to build itself. Maybe we don't want it to do that.

Currently, we match jobs with work elements. How can AI do this?

With employees and current software, as required, we have a way of determining if the employees are doing a good job and the software is doing the correct job. Can and how can AI do this. Do we want it to?

The question is will AI help or hurt the world. The answer is yes, that anything that can be done by people can be done better by AI.

AI systems before release should be tested and the government should govern the testing.

Is AI available for free. Many small, perhaps elementary in nature are free, but many are just applications that can do unique things. No big enterprise systems that are free are known.

Who would own AI systems/ Probably a company or university would have a patent. The output may be important for getting a patent.

Would or could AI end the world? It is not likely, but allowing AI to make life or death decisions would be a risk.

Will AI replace people in some jobs? Yes, for some jobs, a computer could currently do better in many jobs.

Emotions are important for many aspects of modern life. Will AI systems have emotions? One scientist says that without emotions we can't have intelligence. We don't exactly what that means; it may be an extraneous remark.

Here's a question. Are we better with a group of smart people be better around a problem be better or worse than no people around and AI solution?

How will be possible to communicate what AI does and infuse it into a modern system

Does anyone own AI? If you put AI into a business, who owns it and the data?

- Will AI do away with schools and universities?
- Is the U.S. the world leader in AI?
- Will AI be used by the government?
- Can AI make predictions about world events? Or, will it be able to?
- Can AI solve the gun problem?
- You can't replace a human in a stage play, so their jobs are secure. However, AI can design the script. It probably does that today, but I saw no evidence of that.

AI can isolate persons in a film, make some changes, and put that person in another firm. This is of major concern. Singing is often dubbed into an actor's part. Sometime it the actor's own voice and other times it is someone else's voice.

Many items in this category are what they call Weak AI. They are actually standalone systems, but exhibit AI qualities.

Many people are concerned about art work. Who owns a piece of art. If a person tells the computer what to do, then it is Weak AI. It the computer tells itself what to do, then it is Strong AI.

If the AI can do something, who tells the AI system when to do it, and what are the characteristics of the artwork. Why would an AI program want to do anything.

Will AI systems have emotions? A lot of life is influenced by emotions.

Will AI write books? Where does the plot come from? The design of characters is of great importance. Where does this come from?

What will AI systems do on the weekend? A lot of the economy is a result of weekend activity.

Will AI play a game of professional football? Who will tell the AI coaches what strategy to use?

How will AI influence the food industry? Will AI know what to grow? How would AI grow something?

AI Ontology

The subject of ontology is the study of the categories of things that exist or may exist in some domain. The product of such a study, also called ontology, is a catalog of the types of things that are assumed to exist in a domain of interest **D** from the perspective of a person who uses the language **L** for the purpose of talking about **D**. The types in the ontology represent the predicates, word senses, or concept and relation types of the language **L** when used to discuss topics in the domain **D**. (Sowa, 2000)

It is possible to summarize the current state of the art in Modern Artificial Intelligence in one paragraph, followed by more definitive information, as required. Most of the activity is taking place in universities and small companies. The only big gun in the area is IBM that has incredible experience in research, engineering, and marketing. This doesn't mean that there isn't intelligent and experienced people working on it, but when we get down to business, artificial intelligence is a service to mankind and experience goes a long way. There is a tremendous amount of hype surrounding generative AI. Organizations of all sizes are rushing to control the transformative possibilities and the marketing potential. Generative AI will used to enhance large language models to power subsequent generative AI. Capabilities in the following categories will be required to leverage AI: language and image related capability, natural language processing, document understanding, capability of content search, summarization, and system augmentation. In order to streamline tasks and processes, efficient and advanced decision making are required. Things will have to be done differently in the following areas: quantity and quality of data, domain specific models, high quality data processing, the use of the best technologies, and the use of automated business processes. Jobs of tomorrow will be different and the manner in which people work and their skill set will be different. Narrowly defined jobs will be modified through hybrid and remote work. Employee experience will be key and a high percentage of job descriptions haven not yet be defined.

Ontology Knowledge Models

In the future, AI systems will be used to enhance their very selves. This will be achieved through machine learning and through the use of ontologies to delineate new systems. A knowledge base will be used to store the ontologies and machine learning data and that knowledge will be codified as:

Object -> Thesaurus -> Taxonomy

Often, a parent/child relationship will exist of the following form:

Equivalence -> Hierarchical -> Associative

An ontology will be used to represent a total application. An AI system will probably use many AI projects, that will be established with marketable software. With AI, this is supposed to be done by the development software that analyzes the application domain and yields an operational system.

There aren't many situations that exist to serve as an explanatory model. One of the recent books on the concept us The AI-Powered Enterprise: Harness the Powers of Ontologies to Make Your Business Smarter, Faster, and More Profitable, authored by Seth Early, the founder and CEO of an early third-generation AI application on the subject.

Data Ontology

A data ontology is a method for listing a collection of elements with different structures. Data ontologies are a means of organizing data. A data ontology describes a structure and not values.

Semantic Web

In a semantic web, the data elements of concern have a "collected" structure with an inherent flexibility in contrast to a set of database tables and facilitative vocabularies, taxonomies, thesauruses, maps, logic models, and conventional databases. A semantic web provides human readable data.

A data ontology is used to organize data for a particular application domain.

Ontology Advantages

A data ontology provides a description of data elements and their relationships and reflects the structure of an AI system. Accordingly, a data ontology performs like a human brain – at least, that at least one mode of reserve contends. Examples are not readable available.

Deep Learning

The use of an ontology structure facilitates four types of learning in an AI application: deep learning, supervised machine learning, unsupervised machine learning, and a reinforcement machine learning. There is a form of organization inherent in the structure of the various components:

AI system -> Machine learning -> Deep learning

With data science interacting with data elements of all three areas.

AI Ethics

Aristotle's Ethics
The method of achieving effective action or condition.

Analytic Philosophy
The proper method to resolve definitively the problems that ae within the domain of philosophy.

Analytic and Synthetic Clauses
Analytic truths can be true by intuition or pure reason. Synthetic – not by reason.

Attribute Bases Access Control (ABAC)
Access control that relies on the use of subject, object, and control rules.

Autonomy
Capacity of self-determination.

Consequentialism
Consequences of an action that something brought about.

Ethics

The form of philosophy that involves systematizing, defending, and recommending concepts of right or wrong.

Evolutionary Ethics
Ethical concepts that bridge the gap between philosophy and natural science.

Functionalism
Elements are identified by what they do rather than what they are made of.

Logic Atomism
Propositions are built out of elements corresponding to the basic constituents of the world, as sentences are built of words. A statement has meaning if and only it can be verified.

Particularism
The particular features of a situation, and not some general principle or rule determines what conduct is morally right.

Propositional Logic
The branch of logic that studies ways of joining and/or modifies entire propositions made of sentences.

We can't tell a developer what to do, but using these principles, they can effectively address the following pillars of AI development.

AI Deep Learning and Other Things

Most people in the AI world think that machine learning is the future of computer development, because it essentially controls engineering, design, customer service, banking, finance, manufacturing, education, and a myriad of other areas of development.

Brain cells, billions of interconnected neurons make up our nervous system, allow us to think and take action, that is, to do something. Consider, for example, the cerebral cortex that is the outer surface of the brain is grey in color. Most of the brain is white. White is responsible for transmitting information over long distance and storing information. The neurons have a white fatty coating that accelerates the speed of the movement of signals. White matter acts like a highway. Connections slow it down. When eye gets a signal, for example, sent to the cortex that sends the signal in to the brain and you respond like you have seen something. It is a complicated thing.

In the brain, these neurons are packaged in an outer coating called the soma. It contains a nucleus along with some other things to make connections. The neurons are connected together with a long stringy thing call then axon. A neuron has a bunch of receiving ports called then dendrites. Each neuron is only a connecting device; it is a little box like your age or something like that. There are billions of neutrons connected every which way to respond with a signal that makes you do something like remember something or move your arm to tell your heart to do something.

The brain does a lot by the way it responds. Computer scientists took the concept as a way of storing information in a similar connecting device called a neural network. A neural network has a set of starting points and ending points. In between, there are several layers of points that are connected every which way. Each of these points is called a cell. One of these cells, for example, takes a bunch of inputs and modifies them and generates to the next layer. The network of cells can be adjusted to behave in a particular way to give the desired output. That is machine learning. It is exceedingly complicated, but exceedingly useful. It is a big part of artificial intelligence. There are a lot of references to this, and two of the best are: Russell, S. and Norvig, P., *Artificial Intelligence: A Modern Approach*; and Krohn, J., Beylev, and Geld, A., *Deep Learning Illustrated: A Visual, Interactive Guide* to Artificial Intelligence. The Russell and Norvig is one of the best books ever written in the opinion of the author.

AI Regulation

People are afraid of AI, because the computer industry is just keeps barreling along without providing rationale as to what and why they are doing all of this AI stuff. The AI community has such a big ego that they think the world will automatically love what they are doing. Some of the technical advantages produced are first-rate and developed with the considerations that are important to people and business and government. Some of the output of the AI community has no consideration for the people it effects. People are confused and afraid.

Job security
Creating entirely new professions
Reshaping the labor market
Increasing productivity

Seismic shift in the creative arts (art, music, writing, including photography)
Revolutionizing healthcare
Negative employment

AI flaws
Systemic problems
Facial recognition
Discrimination
Complexity of factual information and computer software flaws
Emotion susceptibilities and exploitation
Fakes and forgeries
AI deception
Identification and protection

Personal fears
Strong AI
Ethics
Singularity
    Reliability
    Explain-ability
    Security
Privacy

END OF CHAPTER TWENTY-TWO

Chapter 23

Ontology of Artificial Intelligence Architecture

An artificial intelligence architecture is a specification of the information, computational elements, people, and underlying concepts in a services system. Accordingly, an associated data architecture is a specification of how data is stored, processed, and used in a system of record. A given data architecture effectively governs the flow of data in a system and establishes a relationship between an organization's processes and it's supporting information systems. Data architecture for an enterprise describes its applications, hardware, networks, business objects, business processes, and data. As such, it encompasses a complex set of definitions, methods, data types, and relationships. This paper introduces the concept of *ontology* applied to information systems and describes the essential elements of data architecture.

Ontology

In philosophy, ontology is the study of being (or existence), describes the basic categories, and defines the entities and classes of elements in its domain. In the area of information systems, it is a specification of conceptualization used to enable knowledge sharing and reuse. More specifically, an ontology can be viewed as a data model that describes objects, classes, attributes, and relations. In his ground-breaking book on knowledge representation, John F. Sowa gives an appropriate definition for our purposes:

> The subject of *ontology* is the study of the *categories* of things that exist or may exist in some domain. The product of such a study, called an *ontology*, is a catalog of the types of things that are assumed to exist in a domain of interest ***D*** from the perspective of a person who uses the language ***L*** for the purpose of talking about ***D***. The types in the ontology represent the *predicates, word senses,* or *concept and relation types* of the language ***L*** when used to discuss topics in the domain ***D***. (Sowa, 2000)

One common approach to the delineation of ontological elements is to divide the extant entities into groups called "categories." These lists of categories are quite different from another. It is in this latter sense that ontology is applied to such fields as theology, information science, and artificial intelligence. (Wikipedia 2007)

Ontological Engineering

Ontological engineering encompasses a set of activities conducted during conceptualization, design, implementation, and deployment of ontologies. Ontological engineering seeks to achieve the following goals in a given domain:

Definition of terms
Establishment of a body of domain knowledge
Specification of coherent and expressive knowledge bases

In short, an ontology defines the vocabulary of a problem domain and a set of constraints on how terms are related. It also gives data types and operations defined over the data types.

Data Architecture

Data architecture describes how data is processed, stored, and utilized in a given system. It provides criteria for data processing operations that make it possible to design data flows and also control the flow of data in the system. (Wikipedia, *op. cit.*) Stephens defines data architecture as a corporation's expression of strategy for creating and managing the use of data in order to transform data into information. He goes on to note that it is a strategic asset that must assure the following:

Standardization of data structures
Definition protection of the data resource
Consistence and quality of the data resource
Judicial use of corporate resources
Delivery of timely and credible data
It addresses business needs
That it can be managed in a corporate environment

The fact that data architecture is a "grey architecture" does not detract from its validity.

Business Objects

A *business object* encapsulates the business logic of a single business entity and the data pertinent to that entity. [6] Each business object consists of one or more service components and one or more data components. A *service component* is the functionality supplied by a business object. A *data component* encapsulates data stored in a database.

Accordingly, data architecture is conceptualized as a set of business objects.

Frameworks

A *framework* is a taxonomy for looking at a class of computer applications. It effectively works by identifying the pieces that constitute an application and prescribing how they should be put together. Typically, a framework emphasizes segmentation and sharing at the data level. Operational and reference data are separated, so that reference data may be shared among frameworks. Rather than viewing an application as a monolithic structure supporting a particular business function, it is useful to view an application framework as a collection of one or more of the following elements: a computational engine, a data management component, application building blocks, and a user-interface module. This viewpoint recognizes and takes advantage of off-the-shelf components. The needed infrastructure includes a reference data architecture and a metadata repository. A *reference data architecture* is a prescription of how data should flow within a single application framework and between diverse application frameworks. A *metadata repository* is the concept that allows middleware to transfer data between platforms on a scheduled or dynamic basis.

A framework can be conceptualized as a collection of three views: organization, business, and technical. The *business view* is significant and consists of data, function, workflow, and the solution structure. Within this view, the *data* refers to the operational and historical databases, the legacy files, the staging database, and the transfer files. The *function* denotes the applications and the programs that transfer data between applications. The *workflow* refers to the behavioral aspects of the combination of data and function. The *solution structure* is the data architecture that holds information about the combination of generic components from the data, function, and workflow areas.

Application Domains and Application Groups

An *application domain* (AD) is a suite of application programs, user interfaces, databases, reporting facilities, file, data marts, and related entities that collectively perform an enterprise function. An example would be "Order Management and Trading." In an application domain, all applications are related but some applications are more related than others. Related ADs communicate with each other through a *virtual data exchange* (VDE). The notion of a VDE stems from the need to avoid the case where ADs communicate directly. A set of ADs connected by a VDE are called an *application group* (AG). An example of an AG would be "Investment Operations," perhaps consisting of the following ADs: Order Management and Trading, Holdings Management, Investment Accounting, Custody Processing, and Back Office Integration.

The primary benefit of this viewpoint is that an application group maintains its autonomy while participating in the overall enterprise design through the reference data architecture.

Data Architecture Ontology

The preceding sections give the context for the ontology of data architecture. This section gives definitions for the ontological elements, as listed in Table 1.

Data view is a collection of single elements, such as name, address, order number, etc. Data elements are commonly structured for storage and retrieval purposes and are normally associated with an application or a database, requiring an appropriate semantic context.

Information view is data to which knowledge has been applied. This view incorporates an appropriate semantic definition and represents a "business view" of data. Information is commonly aggregated for analysis, inference, understanding, and decision making.

Data architecture reflects the structure of storage components and the manner in which data is exchanged between them. Data architecture also defines how data will be managed, organized, stored, transformed, accessed, and otherwise made available to applications and users. Data architecture is composed of conceptual-level and logical-level descriptions and derives its applicability through a framework.

Conceptual-level data architecture defines design constructs, known as templates and best use principles concerning their use. It also describes standards, policies, and processes for use of subject data elements.

Logical-level data architecture applies the conceptual constructs and processes to an application domain, and establishes and incorporates data management structures and technology.

A **Framework** is a collection of components, connections, actors, and use cases that comprise a reusable design of a data architecture for a class of business problems. A framework works with a subject data model to establish a context for a data architecture.

Information architecture represents the business-process view of a data architecture, and delineates the information needed to support different business processes. A framework is used to relate technology to users, information structures, and use cases.

Enterprise data architecture is a conceptual-level data architecture that is reusable across the enterprise. This element facilitates data sharing business units and enables risk avoidance and cost reduction.

Subject data model is a high-level view of data with a business perspective, and represents an aggregate view of information from multiple application systems. This data model supports a CRUD matrix integration of application and infrastructure.

Operational database is an online system that usually supports transaction processing and supports operational queries and update capability by being "current" data valued and subject oriented.

Data warehouse is a historical database that is organized for efficient updating from source systems. It may incorporate aggregation and summarization to support upstream data marts. A data warehouse may also allow access/reporting but is not usually optimized for that.

Data mart is a historical database optimized for access and reporting around a business unit. It is usually updated from a data warehouse via "batch updates."

Metadata is a common repository of "data about data" that is sharable between applications and platforms, reflecting business semantics and data sharing.

Staging database is a focal point for data cleansing operations on dynamic data from operational databases.

Data exchange is an event driven platform for exchanging data between applications.

Data hub is a middleware system designed to move data between source and target systems. The source and target systems include operational databases, legacy files, and data warehouse/mart data stores.

Reference data architecture refers to goal-state architecture, enterprise data warehouse, department data mart, and reporting systems.

Collectively, the definitions provide a means of communicating in the problem domain of data architecture.

TABLE 1. Ontological Elements

Number	Element
1	Data View
2	Information View
3	Data Architecture
4	Conceptual-Level Data Architecture
5	Logical-Level Data Architecture
6	Framework
7	Information Architecture
8	Enterprise Data Architecture
9	Subject Data Model
10	Operational Database
11	Data Warehouse
12	Data Mart
13	Metadata
14	Staging Database
15	Data Exchange
16	Data Hub
17	Reference Data Architecture

Ongoing Development

Future developments would include a functional description of each of the ontological elements

END NOF CHAPTER TWENTY-THREE

CHAPTER 24

Just in Case

Well, just in case you are sick and tired with all of this doing, not doing, going, not going, remembering and not remembering, and want to just sit back and enjoy the day, here is something kind of fun for you. You can copy it if you want to:

The Window

Now why would anyone write about one of the most common things in the modern world: a window. After all, there are windows all over the place, and many of them don't have anything covering them up. Probably, there is an interest in windows – especially open ones – because there is almost always a sort of mystery associated with a window. There is natural inclination to find out what's going on. Is it something new and challenging, is it something drastic, is it something that is exceedingly happy or terribly sad?

Try to conceptualize strolling in the country side and coming upon an older building with blown out open windows, what is the first thing you think? Probably it is that no one cares. But that is not necessarily true. Perhaps the owner has passed away and just does not know that the beloved structure with damaged windows is in need of repair. Does caring end with death? Well, that is an open item. It seems that life in the modern world is nothing more than an ever-expanding set of open items. Back to the wide world of windows.

It is entirely possible that there were never any covers of any kind over the rectangular "holes in a proverbial wall". The place was simply not finished, a commonplace consequence for a variety of everyday reasons. What about the windows in some of those middle-eastern homes. It seems as though they typically don't have anything covering the windows – at least that's how they are portrayed in the daily news. Probably it is easier to shoot through an open window and even an open door. That pertains to inside out and is likely true of outside in.

Modern office buildings are frequently designed to be window friendly and look like walls of glass. Obviously there are supporting structures placed in strategic locations to support the whole thing. They are certainly hot in summer and cold in winter giving a lot of work for heating and air conditioning people and also window washers, in addition to window covers and stuff like that.

A thing that some people apparently do is look into other people's windows to see what is going on. The first assumption made in this case is that the objective is to look at the people in hope of seeing something juicy. But how juicy can it really be? Probably, the objective for a good number of inside lookers – called peeping toms – is simply to see how the decorations look. Illegal activity is another thing that is too complicated for words.

Now looking out of a window could also be pretty interesting since windows are up a bit and a person can see farther out. So that brings up an unusual question. Why don't artistic painters depict scenes from a raised position? Of course, some do but not many. Practically everything that one could think of has been done – somewhere in the vast world – even painting a window scape.

There are many additional sorts of windows, many of them. What about the windows associated with computers. An electronic display device is used for input and output on most modern computers, as well as tablets and smart phones. In fact, it is common to see windows inside of windows, and so forth. Millions of dollars are regularly spent by electrical engineers designing display technology enabling windows to be brighter and more readable. Practically everyone knows these days that a piece of software called an operating system is needed to use a computer and that includes phones and tablets, including music players and games. There is a major one called Windows produced by the Microsoft Corporation and the name is trademarked.

Motor vehicles have windows to see out of. The main window is called the windshield that also blocks the wind when moving. Some early cars and trucks did not have wind shields and the driver and front passenger had to wear goggles, much like airplane pilots. In vehicles, there are also side windows, a rear window, and a top window sometimes referred to as a sun roof or a moon roof. Usually the top roof opens for added pleasure. Lately, it has become common to have the top roof cover the entire roof. It is called a panoramic roof. Here is an amazing observation. It is commonplace, especially in Florida and California, to see people riding along the motor ways with the top down. Do you remember seeing someone riding along with the sun roof open?

Have you been downtown lately? Maybe not, but major retail stores have splashy windows, usually around holidays. The main idea is to put people into the holiday mood so they come and buy stuff that they probably do not need to buy, at least at the moment. It seems as though, however, that it is a bit more than that. It's a competition. Which store has the best windows? In this instance, it is not the window, per se, but what is displayed behind the window. Typically, the store will feature pleasing and esthetically appropriate items to showcase. There are even businesses that will prepare windows for a fee, but the pleasure is often in the doing in addition to the result.

Have you ever ridden in an airplane? If you have, then you can guess what this paragraph is going to be all about. If you're lucky, you had the experience of flying in a private jet. Most people say it is pure pleasure. But why? You will soon find out. In the past, commercial air travel was a pleasure. You checked your luggage at the curb and proceeded forthwith to check in at the counter. The passenger space was ample and a meal was usually served if flight time permitted it. If you were fortunate enough to travel first class, you enjoyed orange juice or champagne when you got to your seat that was also first class. During flight, it used to be interesting to look out to see what is going on, and the seats and windows were aligned to facilitate this form of activity. Well, those days are long gone. In order to maximize revenue, airlines have stuffed many seats into a space that was limited to start with, so that a real window is unlikely. Airplane builders have come up with a new kind of window; a window that is not a window, but a computer screen showing an outside scene. The seats and windows are still not aligned, but passengers do not care after they go through check in.

Welcome to "Windows of the World". You've undoubtedly seen a sign like that, somewhere in this vast country. As mentioned, if you can think it, then it probably exists. Scenic attractions commonly view their services as a window to something fun, enjoyable, and worthy of your attention. A good book is a window to whatever the book contains. Hundreds of "Windows to ..." can easily be imagined.

An interval of time can also be regarded as a window, as in "You have a time window of three days to get to the west coast". Almost anything that is time dependent can be expressed in terms of a window. Moreover, anything you can see through is a window, even though it may be on the floor or the ceiling. Most windows are rectangular, although some are round, square, and all sorts of shape.

So just what is the window and just what is the something that is not a window. A window has been defined as an opening in a wall to allow light, air, or just about anything else to get in. If you break a hole in the side of a barn that allows in light, air, dust, and all manners of bugs, have you created a window? Most people would class that as a nasty hole in the wall. Not a window. Many people say that anything you can see through is a window, even though it may be on the floor or the ceiling. Most windows are rectangular, although some are round, square, and all sorts of shape. To finish the definition of a window, it is an opening with casements or sashes that contain transparent material, such as glass or plastic, capable of being open or closed. A glass window that can't be opened and an opaque window are still windows. Some windows are classed by what they do for people. But a window, per se, does not really do anything. It just sits there, looking kind of stupid. A ticket window is used to distribute tickets, so to speak, to customers who use the same facility to obtain them. But, isn't that exactly what most things in the world do. They kind of sit there looking kind of stupid for other people to use.

It's getting a little cool in here so I'll close the window.

Author: Harry Katzan, Jr.
Copyright 2024 Harry Katzan, Jr.
All rights reserved.
You may copy this. Attribution would be appreciated.

END OF CHAPTER TWENTY-FOUR

The Library

This section of the book is a brief sidelight that gives a bibliography of titles where the information in the various chapters came from. In all cases the information has been paraphrased from its original source. The books are all written by the author of this book. Several of the books have been reprinted and combined as duologies or trilogies. The reason is that some publishers just charge more for their books than many people want to pay. It is just that simple. The titles vary for copyright reasons. *The primary reference always comes first for each entry.* If you want to read more about a subject, you can look in the following references. The books are readily available from Amazon.

Return to Inaction (Chapter 1)
The Romeo Affair, Authors Tranquility, 2023
Retired Old Men Eating Out, iUniverse, 2023
Up, Down and Anywhere, Westwood, 2023 (A duology)

How About the Romeo Club (Chapter 2)
The Romeo Affair, Authors Tranquility, 2023
Retired Old Men Eating Out, iUniverse, 2023
Up, Down and Anywhere, Westwood, 2023 (A duology)

Interesting Events (Chapter 3)
The Romeo Affair, Authors Tranquility, 2023
Retired Old Men Eating Out, iUniverse, 2023
Up, Down and Anywhere, Westwood, 2023 (A duology)

The General (Chapter 4)
The Day After the Night Before, iUniverse, 2022
Everything is Good, Westwood, 2022
Journey of Matt and the General, Authors Tranquility, 2023

The Queen (Chapter 5)
The Day After the Night Before, iUniverse, 2022
Everything is Good, Westwood, 2022
Journey of Matt and the General. Authors Tranquility, 2023

Taking a Look at Matt (Chapter 6)
The Day After the Night Before, iUniverse, 2022
Everything is Good, Westwood, 2022
Journey of Matt and the General, Authors Tranquility, 2023

The Rescue (Chapter 8)
The Day After the Night Before, iUniverse, 2022
Everything is Good, Westwood, 2022
Journey of Matt and the General, Authors Tranquility, 2023

The Escape (Chapter 9)
The Day After the Night Before, iUniverse, 2022
Everything is Good, Westwood, 2022
Journey of Matt and the General, Authors Tranquility, 2023

The Royal Baby (Chapter 10)
The Mysterious Case of the Royal Baby, iUniverse, 2019
The Royal Baby, Westwood, 2023
Included in The Magnificent Monarchy, iUniverse, 2022 (A trilogy)

The Royal Marriage (Chapter 11)
The Curious Case of the Royal Marriage, iUniverse, 2019
The Royal Marriage, Westwood, 2023
Included in The Magnificent Monarchy, iUniverse, 2022 (A trilogy)

The General and Royal Family (Chapter 12)
The Auspicious Case of the General and the Royal Family, iUniverse, 2019
The General and Royal Family, Westwood, 2023
Included in The Magnificent Monarchy, iUniverse, 2022 (A trilogy)

The Virus (Chapter 13)
The Virus, iUniverse, 2020
Included in Worldwide Trouble, iUniverse, 2022 (A trilogy)

The Pandemic (Chapter 14)
The Pandemic, iUniverse, 2020
Included in Worldwide Trouble, iUniverse, 2022 (A trilogy)

From Russia with Love (Chapter 15)
Life is Good, iUniverse, 2020
The Good Life, Westwood, 2021
Included in The Good Life and Discovery, Westwood, 2023 (A duology)

From Outer Space with Love (Chapter 16)
The Tale of Discovery, iUniverse, 2021
The Discovery, Westwood, 2022
Included in The Good Life and Discovery, Westwood, 2023 (A duology)

The Terrorist Event (Chapter 17)
The Terrorist Plot, iUniverse, 2021
The Terrorists: Mission Failed, Westwood, 2023

An Information Leak (Chapter 18)
The Untimely Situation, iUniverse, 2021
An Unexpected Happening, Westwood, 2023

Ransomware (Chapter 19)
The Untimely Situation, iUniverse, 2021
An Unexpected Happening, Westwood, 2023

And That's the End of the Story (Chapter 20)
The Day After the Night Before, iUniverse, 2022
Everything is Good, Westwood, 2022
Journey of Matt and the General, Authors Tranquility, 2023

Artificial Intelligence (Chapter 21)
Another Romeo Affair, Author's Tranquility, 2023
Retired Old Men Eating Out, iUniverse, 2023
Up, Down and Anywhere, Westwood, 2023

Thinking About Artificial Intelligence (Chapter 22)
On the Trail of Artificial Intelligence, iUniverse, 2023

Ontology of Artificial Intelligence Architecture (Chapter 23)
On the Trail of Artificial Intelligence, iUniverse, 2023

Just in Case (Chapter 24)
The Day After the Night Before, iUniverse, 2022

END OF THE LIBRARY

About This Novel

This is a book of fiction and is intended for the entertainment of the reader. The main characters, that is, Matt, the General, Ashley, Anna, Mark Clark, Buzz Bunday, the retired Queen, academic and medical personnel, employees, and support persons are totally made up to suit the novel.

All references to aircraft, pilots, and procedures are all made up for the occasion. Some references may be true or correct, as the case may be, but only by accident. They are foremost in my imagination. The doctors and medical terminology are just imagined, and anything medical is just made up from reading the Internet. Any reference to doctor's conventions and procedures are imagined.

My wife Margaret proof read the manuscript for spelling and other errors and did a magnificent job of it. Our daughter Kathryn helped me whenever necessary and did so with great pleasure. They are wonderful inspiration.

Thanks for reading the book. The book follows the usual procedure of no violence, no sex, and no bad language. It is accessible to readers of all ages.

ABOUT THIS NOVEL

[illegible]

ABOUT THE AUTHOR

Harry Katzan, Jr. is a professor who has written several books and many papers on computers and service, in addition to some novels. He has been an advisor to the executive board of a major bank and a general consultant on various disciplines. He and his wife have lived in Switzerland where he was a banking consultant and a visiting professor. He is an avid runner and has completed 94 marathons including Boston 13 times and New York 14 times. He holds bachelors, masters, and doctorate degrees.

BOOKS BY HARRY KATZAN, JR.

Computers and Information Systems

Advanced Programming
APL Programming and Computer Techniques
APL Users Guide
Computer Organization and the System/370
A PL/I Approach to Programming Languages
Introduction to Programming Languages
Operating Systems
Information Technology
Computer Data Security
Introduction to Computer Science
Computer Systems Organization and Programming
Computer Data Management and Database Technology
Systems Design and Documentation
Microprogramming Primer
The IBM 5100 Portable Computer
Fortran 77
The Standard Data Encryption Algorithm
Introduction to Distributed Data Processing
Distributed Information Systems
Invitation to Pascal
Invitation to Forth
Microcomputer Graphics and Programming Techniques
Invitation to Ada
Invitation to Ada and Ada Reference Manual
Invitation to Mapper
Operating Systems (2nd Edition)
Local Area Networks
Invitation to MVS (with D. Tharayil)
Introduction to Computers and Data Processing
Managing Uncertainty
Privacy, Identity, and Cloud Computing

Business and Management

Multinational Computer Systems
Office Automation
Management Support Systems
A Manager's Guide to Productivity, Quality Circles, and Industrial Robots
Quality Circle Management
Service and Advanced Technology

Service Science

A Manager's Guide to Service Science
Foundations of Service Science
Service Science
Introduction to Service
Service Concepts for Management
A Collection of Service Essays
Hospitality and Service

Little Books

The Little Book of Artificial Intelligence
The Little Book of Service Management
The Little Book of Cybersecurity
The Little Book of Cloud Computing
The Little Book of Managing Uncertainty

Novels

The Mysterious Case of the Royal Baby
The Curious Case of the Royal Marriage
The Auspicious Case of the General and the Royal Family
A Case of Espionage
Shelter in Place
The Virus
The Pandemic
Life is Good
The Vaccine
A Tale of Discovery
The Terrorist Plot
An Untimely Situation
The Final Escape
Everything is Good
The Good Life (reprint of Life is Good)
The Discovery (reprint of A Tale of Discovery)
The Good Life and Discovery (Duology)
The Romeo Affair
Another Romeo Affair
Here, There and Everywhere
Up, Down and Anywhere
The Last Adventure

Little Books

The Little Book of Artificial Intelligence
The Little Book of Service Management
The Little Book of Cybersecurity
The Little Book of Cloud Computing
The Little Book of Managing Uncertainty

Advanced Novel

The Day After the Night Before
The Journey of Matt and the General
(a reprint of The Day After the Night Before

Trilogies

The Magnificent Monarchy
Worldwide Trouble
Winning is Good

END OF BOOKS BY HARRY KATZAN JR.

END OF THIS BOOK

Printed in the USA
CPSIA information can be obtained
at www.ICGtesting.com
LVHW011408190324
774567LV00010BA/350

9 781963 636598